BOUNDLESS AND BARE

BOUNDLESS AND BARE

A. MADHAVAN

Translated from the Tamil by Sandhya Raman

ZERO DEGREE PUBLISHING

Original in Tamil, A. Madhavanin Sirukathaigal © A . Madhavan 2019
English Translation, Boundless and Bare : Sandhya Raman
English Translation © Zero Degree Publishing
First Edition: December 2019

ISBN: 978-93-88860-27-7
ZDP title no: 27

ZERO DEGREE PUBLISHING
No.55(7), R Block, 6th Avenue,
Anna Nagar,
Chennai - 600 040

Website: www.zerodegreepublishing.com
E Mail id: zerodegreepublishing@gmail.com
Phone : 98400 65000

Cover Art by Bianca Joseph
Typeset by Vidhya Velayudham

Publishers' Note

Writers are the cultural identity, the memory of the aeon, the conscience and the voice of the society. By the sheer magic of their art, they surpass the barriers of language, land and culture. Any country should pride itself on possessing writers – national assets – whose works in translation have the potential to catapult them into international renown.

The Latin American Boom during the 1960s and '70s was a launchpad era that thrust names such as Julio Cortázar, Gabriel García Márquez, Carlos Fuentes, Jorge Luis Borges and Mario Vargas Llosa into the Anglophone literary world where they enjoyed a plausive reception.

Publication of translated nineteenth-century Russian literature fetched Tolstoy and Chekhov iconic status. Due to the availability of and the demand for their works in translation, Haruki Murakami of Japan and Orhan Pamuk of Turkey have become bestselling writers to watch in the present day and age.

What we understand from all of this is that translation and publication are fruitful endeavors that engage national writers and their oeuvres with the world at large and vice versa.

Zero Degree Publishing aims to introduce to the world some of the finest specimens of modern Indian literature, to begin with, we take great pride in introducing Tamil literature in English translation because, as Henry Gratton Doyle said, "It is better to have read a great work of another culture in translation than never to have read it at all."

– *Gayathri Ramasubramanian & Ramjee Narasiman*

Publishers

Translator's Note

Translation from one language to another requires one to have a proficiency in both the original and the language to be translated in. When translating one should not just render the text in the given language word to word, but transport the reader to world the author originally created.

When Gayathri offered my first novel to be translated for Zero Degree Publishing, I was excited until I read through the book the first time. It was *Kadaitheru Kadhaigal – a collection of short stories by A. Madhavan*. Madhavan though was born in Trivandrum, Kerala wrote most of his books in Tamil. The book is set in late 1800s or early 1900s in Trivandrum, Kerala. The language spoken by the characters in the book was a mix of Tamil and Malayalam owing to the author's geography.

The weight of the work drew upon me as I started translating them into English. Staying true to what the author had envisioned in his stories and to bring out the ethos that the author had penned in his book was quite a challenge. I had to read and re-read the stories to understand what the characters were trying to convey. However, referring language dictionaries and taking the help of others I was able to do justice to the book.

Through the stories, I was able to see the life that Madhavan had depicted in his book with a huge bazaar, the town of Trivandrum, the palace and the roads that surrounded it. I met the vendors, the goats, the shepherd, the local milkman and others who inhabited the streets and lanes surrounding the bazaar.

The imagination of the author describing the lives of the folks in such simple language made for not only an exciting read but interesting to translate as well.

I hope that upon reading the English translation, I am able to transport the reader to the Trivandrum of the Maharajas where Ummini and Paachi are still roaming the streets waiting for Govindan to wake them up early morning each day.

About the Author

A. Madhavan (1934)

One of the forerunners of Tamil Literature, A. Madhavan, was born in Trivandrum, Kerala. His parents were Aavudainayagam and Chellammal who belonged to Kumari district. He completed his school education through Malayalam medium. Though he did not formally study in Tamil, his knowledge and acumen of Tamil Literature is quite extensive.

He has to his credit hundreds of short-stories, three novels and his translated works include *Ini Naan Urangattum, Sanmaanam* which also feature prominently in his literary work.

His work *Ilakkiya Chuvadukal* won him the Sahitya Akademi award in the year 2015.

He weaved stories out of the same bazaar where he lived, which has also earned him the name – *The Bazaar's Artist.*

Eighty Five year old A.Madhavan, currently lives with his family in Trivandrum, Kerala.

Contents

Compensation

"Hey Madasami! It looks like we are going to be empty-handed today as well. I don't see any trader in sight. Today is the fourth day when we had no work. Do you have a *beedi*, by the way?"

"Can't you just mind your own business? I am already irritated and you want my *beedi* also, is it? Why don't you take my life instead? I will be happy."

"Why are you shouting at me now? I am not taking away your job here. I am equally jobless for the last three days. All of us who were brokers in this bazaar are jobless now. Whatever meagre amount we used to earn was enough for just a drink. What remained was for food. At this rate, we won't have any income at all. I think the best option is to leave this broker's job and go to the ship dockyard. Even if we carry loads, there will be a steady income every day."

"If you ever find a job like that, please let me know. Now leave me alone," growled Madasami.

"Hey Madasami, you seem to be very pissed off today. What's the matter with you? Did you have a tussle with your wife this morning? She would have shouted at you. Why wouldn't she? What else will she do when you keep drinking off your earnings every day? How is she supposed to manage the household and feed three stomachs, including that of a hungry seven-year-old?"

"You are building tall tales here, as if I am earning nine hundred rupees every day and am emptying my pockets every day at the bar. It has been so long since I even saw a full day's salary. But to tell you the truth, even she thinks the same of me. I could not take it anymore and had to thrash her last night. Only we know the struggle we go through to earn every rupee. She sits at home and tells me that I am spending my day drinking at the liquor shop and returning home empty-handed. My son Pazhani is growing. He is around eight now. What will he think of me if she asks such a question before him? He will go and tell his friends in school that his father is an alcoholic. He is such a brat and a monkey without a tail. I am stuck with these two for life. Here, take this, buy a bundle of *beedis* and come. Let us go near the bazaar centre with all the big stores. It is almost noon and we still haven't made any money."

Dhanu took the money from Madasami and walked to the shop. But before he could turn the corner, a school boy on a cycle braked and screeched to a halt next to him.

"Who is the jewel broker Madasami here? Do you know him? Will you be able to take me to him?" he asked urgently.

"Wait, wait! Why do you need Madasami now? Do you need to sell some silver or gold? Give it to me and I will sell it for you at a very good price. What do you have to sell?" Dhanu looked at him up and down.

"I am not here to sell anything. While returning from school we were coming by the road around the tank. They were laying the road and Madasami's son fell into a barrel of boiling tar. I was told that his father Madasami will be here. I came as fast as I could."

As soon as Dhanu heard this, his mind and body went numb. He composed himself and asked, "He fell into the tar barrel? Was it boiling hot? How is he now?"

"Yes, it was boiling hot. When I left the place, they said that he might not survive. Are you Madasami?"

"No. Come with me quickly. I will show you." Dhanu half walked, half ran towards Madasami with the boy following on his cycle. Seeing them approach, Madasami thought it was someone trying to sell something and walked towards them.

But as soon as he heard the news, he jumped up and down as if he had fallen in the boiling tar and ran towards his son with the boy giving directions. The brokers with whom Madasami had been talking followed them.

"Pazhani, I told you a million times not to go anywhere. Why didn't you listen to me? You could not come home straight after school. You had to go around to play. Had I known something like this would happen, I would not have let you go anywhere. I would have tied your hands and legs and kept you safe," wept Madasami's wife Panjali.

"Will you just shut your mouth? He has gone. He is not going to come back just because you wail now. I am also suffering here. I am not even out with my gang drinking until I am senseless. If only you had seen his body, your heart would have stopped beating that very instant. At the hospital, the doctors conducted his autopsy and gave me half his body with all his organs removed. They had just stitched him up and wrapped him in a leaf. I had to take whatever was left of him to the crematorium. Imagine breaking a big beautiful vase and trying to put it together with half the pieces."

"Oh please! Don't tell me all that! My heart is going to stop just by listening to your words. Even though I could not give him rice and luxury every day, I was able to feed him gruel daily. Whether I had anything to eat or not, I made sure he never went hungry. He was the life of this house. What can I do to bring back my son? I wonder how much he suffered before dying."

"If you don't stop wailing and shut your mouth, I am leaving."

"Where are you going now? Even now you want to leave me alone? What is it that you have in the bazaar? Do you even know how many days it has been since you brought money home? I don't even remember the last time I had food. I wish the Gods had taken away my life instead of my son's."

"Will you just shut up now? You want to die? I am going to find a way for that. Today is Thursday. It has been four days since our son passed away. I haven't gone to the bazaar in the last four days. Moreover, the government had promised some compensation for our son. I have to go and inquire about that. If I also sit and cry with you, who is going to do all this? Who is going to earn for the house?"

"Whoever was earning for this house until now shall earn. We had only one child and now he is gone. Will the government bring him back? Or will the money compensate for the life of our son? Don't you have even an iota of sorrow that you are willing to take the money for our son's blood? Are you shameless?"

"Hey Panjali! Shut your mouth or I will kill you with my hands. Stay here and keep howling. I am leaving."

When Madasami left the house and walked on the road, he stumbled; his heart felt heavy and he started speaking to himself:

Pazhanichami, the boy who made me a father, will not call me again. He was hardly eight years old and mischievous too. After a lot of struggle, we were able to get him admitted to school. During the entire first grade, his mother used accompany him to and from school. Now he said he had become older and wanted to go on his own. And death followed him. He was very dear at home, especially to his mother. She never liked it when I scolded him, even when he had done any mischief.

When I scolded him, his mother would pounce on me. So I just let him be, thinking the mischief would pass as he grew older. I told him not to go to school. But he wouldn't listen. He wanted the free meal they served and his friends to play with. Even on that day he was returning with his friends. He had overlooked the boiling tar barrel behind the road roller. Little did he or the boy who pushed him realize that this would happen. But it was not the boy who pushed him. It was death. Death had followed him and pushed him into the boiling tar barrel. The boiling tar had oozed into his clothes and had stuck to the skin of his body. He came out of it like a skinned fish. When I saw him on the hospital bed, I realized there was no hope. My heart ached so much that it became numb.

The hospital staff spoke so casually. "Are you the boy's father? The statement here says that it was the negligence of the PWD workers and the boy died on the spot. Sign here. What can we do? If there is life, then death is a part of it. As difficult as it is to accept, we must learn to move on." He said this easily. How could I tell this to my wife? How could I explain it to her? The guy from the department said that they will give a substantial compensation. The boy is gone. My broker's work has no chance of revival now. Whatever the compensation money I get, I will open a small shop with the boy's name and survive the rest of my life. But how will I explain all this to the woman at home? Is he going to wake up and come now if she sits and cries all day? Still, it is the nature of a woman to be soft and tender. Now it is her one and only son who met this horrific end. She will not calm down so easily.

—

When he reached the Taluk office, Madasami was asked to wait for the officer to arrive. He went and sat on the bench outside the office. He felt empty. It was bright and sunny. Across the road in the park stood the statue of Maharaja Chithirai Thirunal. Green city buses, taxis, cyclists, people going to the treasury department, lawyers going to the high court wearing black coats and white pants, all went past him. Madasami sat there, looking at everything without any emotion. Everyone had work to do, some place to be; only he was jobless. He did not have to be anywhere. Someone wearing a watch walked past and he asked for the time. It was half past noon. The officer was yet to arrive. He went and asked the peon again. "Can't you see that he is not there? You will know when he arrives," the peon snarled.

"I guess I have to come back tomorrow. Had I gone to the bazaar, I might have made some money now. Just when I was about to leave the house, that bitch said something negative. Let me see if I can still earn a rupee or two for today." With these thoughts, Madasami got up from the bench and started walking.

It was 8 pm when Madasami reached home. His wife, lying on the narrow bench outside the house, got up when she saw him. The oil lamp on the wall was flickering, indicating that it might go off any moment. There was a picture of Swami Ayyappan on the wall. A shirt and shorts of their dead son hung on the rope. Next to it on the wall hung his bag with his writing board and books. An old black sari was lying crumpled in the corner.

"It should be almost eight or nine now. You went early in the morning and are just returning. If you have earned anything, go to the tea shop and buy something for yourself. I didn't light the stove today. I didn't feel like eating anything either."

"I didn't earn anything. I was waiting outside the Taluk office till 1 pm. After that I came to the bazaar. What can I earn if I go at that time? The provision store owner gave me fifty paise. I had tea and the remaining change is in my shirt pocket. I thought you would have cooked something. Didn't you eat anything?"

"Whatever little you earn will be given directly to the tea shop. I had to borrow rice for gruel yesterday. I drank the remaining gruel at noon today. Suddenly my son's face came before my face and even that meagre gruel would not go down my throat. Are you drunk even today? What is the stench?"

"No, why would I drink? I have been out in the sun all day. That is the stench of the sweaty shirt that I just removed."

"Don't I know you? I have been with you for so long. You just need a reason to drink. Now you have your dead son as an excuse."

"Don't just keep talking and ranting whatever you imagine. I will not be quiet for too long."

Panjali didn't utter a word after that. The oil lamp died on its own and the house became dark. She just turned and cried in the corner.

Madasami spent the next eight to ten days walking to the Taluk office until his legs and hips wore out, putting his thumb impression on the documents that were presented to him, talking to people and asking for recommendations, spending his afternoons outside on the bench and finally getting the papers signed by the officer, the ward councilor, and witnesses to the accident. After all this, he got a hundred and twenty rupees as compensation.

"Count and check Madasami. Count it here before you leave the premises. You do not have to give me anything. But I had to come here for your sake three times. Pay the taxi driver fifteen rupees for that alone," said the ward councilor, pointing to the driver. After paying the driver, just as Madasami counted the money and tied it to his waist, the witnesses were waiting for him with broad smiles outside the Taluk office.

"Hey Madasami, you forgot us as soon as you got the money and quietly tied it to your waist. We came here all the way since the last three days leaving our jobs only for you..."

"So how much did I get for that? You are talking as if I got a thousand rupees and am hiding it away from you. Even before I could get hold of the entire amount, the ward councilor asked me to pay his driver. This money would not even cover the candies and sweets I bought for my son in the last eight years. For this meagre amount, I had to walk so long all these days. How many of you are here? Five? Is ten rupees enough for each of you? Are you all satisfied?"

After paying them all, when Madasami counted the money that remained, it was fifty odd rupees. "Fifty rupees! The value of my Pazhanichami is fifty rupees! She told me so many times and tried to stop me so many times. She was against this cheap money. I fought with her and said that they will give a big sum. Fifty rupees!" he ranted.

In the park opposite the Taluk office, a crow sat on top of the king's crown. Madasami came out of the office, walked across the park, crossed the police station, the fort and kept walking. He felt both heavy and empty. When he felt the money in his shirt pocket, he lost his wits.

When he reached the junction after the fort, he stopped. If he turned east and walked he could go to the bazaar. If he turned west he could go home. His mind oscillated. Before he could think further, Madasami's feet walked east.

By the time he reached home, it was late and very dark. Only when he opened the wooden door did Panjali wake to the screeching noise. "Why is it so late? I heard that you got the money today. One of your broker friends came and told me. You should be satisfied now. I lost my son. You got your money. No wonder you are late today. Now let me see the money that paid in compensation for my son's life."

Madasami leaned forward, took a fistful of coins and placed them in the extended hands of Panjali.

"What is this so much change? Is this all? What did you do with the money?" Panjali asked in disbelief.

Madasami, seated at the edge near the door, belched and vomited on the floor with a loud sound.

The stench was unbearable: regurgitated cheap liquor, fish and what not…

It appeared that he had eaten a lot. He looked up at Panjali and vomited again.

"Hey Pazhanichami! Are you looking at this? This is how much your father valued you. This is why he sold you for money!"

Panjali wailed loudly, beating herself on her head and chest. The whole village was engulfed in darkness and her cries were heard clearly into the darkness.

Honour

Veeraiyan was numb. The thought of having to step into a police station was petrifying. His mind went back to his first time in a police station. It was a long time ago, but what happened that night was still vivid in his mind, enough to shake him to his bones. It had been the same Paalayam police station on that fateful night as well. His heart started racing as he recollected...

A couple of years back, Veeraiyan, a porter in the shipyard, had been rounded up along with a few others by cops on night patrol. It had been quite an exhausting day at work and he had decided to sleep on the bench on Bazaar road outside the market. On hot summer nights, it was customary for workers to sleep outdoors.

The cops rounded up those sleeping on public benches and took them into custody. They were asked to sit on the floor and wait for the inspector. A couple of them were pleading to be let off, while Veeraiyan and two others sat down quietly and nodded off. The humidity and heat of the summer made it difficult to stay awake for long. Veeraiyan couldn't sleep, for it was his first time inside a police station. He looked around.

Paalayam town was not a place where serious crime was frequent. It was the only police station from the port to the bazaar. Petty crimes like pickpockets, domestic arguments, fights between neighbours, etc. were the common complaints that the station received. That night, other than the gang of sleepy heads who were nabbed along with Veeraiyan, the cells were empty. There were stacks of files in the cupboard gathering dust. A constable sat outside, put his head against the wall and dozed off.

There were four other constables inside, including the two who had arrested Veeraiyan. One of them was middle-aged. A young boy brought tea and biscuits and the sleeping constable came inside to have his share. They all gathered at the centre table slurping tea while munching on biscuits and laughing. The cop at the centre seemed to be the oldest. He was also the heaviest and had a thick bushy moustache which hid his lips. Seeming to be proud of his moustache, he kept twirling it from time to time, ensuring that the tea and biscuit remnants did not spoil his prized possession. He started recounting yesteryear stories and stories of his bravery, when suddenly there was a commotion outside.

It was past midnight. A drunk guy was dragged inside by a furious cop. He had been drinking in public, and on seeing the cop, he had thrown the liquor bottle in an open drain. The cop wasted no time and nabbed him. It was not just the loss of evidence that angered the cop, but also the loss of free liquor, which he could have shared with his colleagues. Adding fuel to fire was the drunkard's irritating rant. At the station, each of the cops, fresh and energetic after their midnight snack, decided to take turns in thrashing him. They would have probably let him go had he been with his liquor bottle. The heavy cop at the centre table, with drum-like thighs, took a sadistic pleasure in hammering on the drunkard's back, holding his head between his drum-like thighs. They kept punching and thrashing him till they were worn out.

But the drunkard didn't seemed to flinch. Once he realized the cops were fatigued, he went and crashed in a corner as if nothing had happened. For someone who had never been inside a police station before, Veeraiyan had wet his pants out of fear. The inspector returned next morning and all of them were released with a warning.

After that night at the police station, Veeraiyan decided on two things. First, he decided to change his job. A labourer or a porter is seen as just a carrier, not even as a person. Often compared to donkeys that carry loads, they are frequently ill-treated and taken for granted. Second, he decided never to set foot in a police station again.

Until today!

Today, he had to go to the station and answer shameful questions about Parvathy!

He asked himself, "Why Parvathy? Why did she do it? What pushed her to take the decision? Couldn't she have just run away from home?" The more Veeraiyan pondered, the more he couldn't make sense of what had happened to her! His Parvathy! He thought whether it would be fair to say that she still belonged to him? He couldn't bring himself to accept that his wife was no longer alive.

Even when her remains were brought to him by the police for identification, he didn't feel anything.

He couldn't find answers to the innumerable questions that kept buzzing in his head. No matter how many times he thought to himself: "Was it Parvathy who hanged herself? Why didn't she wait for me to reach home? She could have spoken to me." The eerie emptiness of the house, her abandoned clothes and her scent could not convince him that she was actually no more. He lay at night staring into the darkness, convincing himself that she was really gone!

He was shaken out of his thoughts by Shivan *Annachi* [1]. He was like an older brother to the whole community and owned the store in which Veeraiyan worked. Shivan handed him some money and said, "Get up! Get up! No use sitting like this. What has happened cannot be undone. She has gone and we cannot bring her back. Now take this money. Go to the police station and tell them what happened. Don't be scared. Remember! This money is for you. Don't you dare show it to the cops, else your pockets will be emptied. And listen, tell them exactly what happened. Now I have to go to the store. You also get up and go to the police station. Life has to go on!"

Veeraiyan looked at the money and thought, "Shivan *Annachi* has always had a soft corner for me. It's been seven years since I left the Rengapuram community. I would have been alone on the roads if not for him." Veeraiyan mustered his wits and decided to go to the police station for the formalities.

The Paalayam police station was just a mile from the bus stop. On any normal day, Veeraiyan would walk ten times the distance.

But this morning, he was weighed down by sorrow and felt unable to walk the distance. He decided to take the bus and avoid the strenuous walk. For ten paise, he would get down at Madhavaraayar statue and just walk across to the police station. Veeraiyan walked to the bus stop mechanically, like a wound-up toy which goes on, his mind and body unable to think or act voluntarily.

The otherwise buzzing and crowded bus stop seemed almost deserted; only some students on their way to tutorial college and a group of medical college students were waiting. Even the breakfast stand wasn't open yet. The clock hadn't struck eight, else there would be a crowd flocked at the stand. The voice of the lady who owned the stand would be heard over the traffic, just like the frying *pooris'* aroma, which wafted for miles.

The "Hare Rama Hare Krishna" hum was heard from the ashram opposite the bus stand. Swamiji might not be in his ashram, else the hum would have been louder and audible from a distance. The bus stand stank of cow dung and there were flies all over. It reminded him how she used to swab the mud floor of his house with cow dung to keep it clean. Now with Parvathy gone, there were only flies to keep him company. Every thought, everything he saw, took him back to Parvathy. A bus came by. The medical college students boarded the bus, but it did not go to the police station. He decided to wait for his bus for some more time.

A fire engine sped by and turned right on the main road, followed by locals on bicycles. There was always a commotion during a fire accident and the locals would use the commotion to loot whatever they could lay their hands on, just like the folks in *Padhinaalu Muri* [2].

The lads following the fire engine reminded Veeraiyan of the residents of Padhinaalu Muri, who would rather loot, or stand by and gawk, or just gossip, instead of offering to help. Veeraiyan thought to himself, "I should not have gone to that place. Even when I was on the streets and had nowhere to go, I should not have gone to that place. It was just my presumption that cost me Parvathy. She finished her life at the end of a rope." His mind wandered to Parvathy again, like a lump in his throat that would not go down.

Veeraiyan felt his stomach tighten, feeling numb with a familiar sense of déjà vu. With this feeling, he could not decide how to react. He had felt the same when he had met Parvathy for the first time. Their first conversation, first touch, first hug, kiss and their intimate moments, all seemed like they had happened to him earlier. He had often wondered how it was possible when he had never seen Parvathy before. Now all that was left of Parvathy were her ashes.

It has been two years since they had set foot in Padhinaalu Muri, the first place where Veeraiyan decided to set up his own home. Choosing to set out on his own rather than be at the mercy of others was the main reason why he had left Rengapuram community in the first place. All that he had to do at home was to be at the mercy of his father, wash his step-mother's clothes, and be at their beck and call, without aspiring for any personal status or identity. But he would be guaranteed food on his plate and a roof above his head. Even his uncle's son, older to him, had offered a job at a store. Had Veeraiyan accepted that offer, he would have still to be under the scrutiny of his clan. But he did not want such restrictions; he needed his pride and dignity, hence he left his father's house.

He left home and came to the bazaar which offered a ton of opportunities to make a living. Pushing carts, carrying loads and being handy easily earned him a rupee or two at the end of the day. Enough to feed a person. He thought: "I didn't need a luxurious life or a silk shirt. I am happy with just a cotton shirt to cover myself."

In his initial days out of home, Arunachala Reddy had asked about his background and Veeraiyan had replied fluently in Tamil not to give himself away. But Arunachala Reddy, on learning that Veeraiyan also belonged to the Reddy caste, mocked him for being a coolie in the bazaar and carrying loads. "Aren't you the younger brother of the man who works at the garment store? Your father is Kuruva Reddy, right? Why do you want to work like this and bring a bad name to your father?"

Veeraiyan shot back, "What is wrong in what I am doing? I didn't come to you using my father's name or my caste and ask for a job. I didn't come to you begging for money. I don't need your advice, nor am I obliged to you in any manner."

After that, he never went near Sabapathy temple street. Most of the store owners and business people in the bazaar were Reddys. They would try to change his mind using his caste or his father's name. Deciding that he would rather live on the streets than go begging at someone's door, he joined the shipyard as a porter. Honour and dignity were above everything. This went on for not one or two, but for five long years. After this, he met the Reddy with the big moustache who changed his life.

That was the time after his stint at the police station, when he had just quit his job as a porter. Veeraiyan had become a salesman. Selling an assortment of things – combs, pocket mirrors, eye liners, liquid *bindi, sticker bindi,* needles and threads, pins, rat poison, etc. He would go and stand with these at the bus stops and easily earn two rupees profit at the end of the day without anyone's help. Later in the evening, he would buy small aluminium cups in bulk for a very cheap price and sell them along the sidewalks with a fifty paise profit.

He had seen Moustache Reddy at the aluminium shop chatting with the owner a couple of times when he went to buy the cups. No Reddy person usually maintained a moustache. This man had a moustache in the shape of a sickle, thick as a corn cob; it was his identity; he was known throughout the bazaar as "Moustache Reddy."

No one knew his real name or even wanted to. He had been banished from his town because his wife had eloped with someone. However, he never seemed to be bothered by the banishment and never identified himself by his caste. He lived in Padhinaalu Muri in a small hut. As soon as Veeraiyan heard this from the aluminium shop owner during one of his evening visits, Veeraiyan felt immense respect for Moustache Reddy. He was introduced to Reddy by the aluminium shop owner, which later led to his marrying Reddy's daughter Parvathy.

A bus screeched to a halt and Veeraiyan saw the bold letters PAALAYAM. He boarded the bus, took a corner seat and fear surged through him. He pondered over what Shivan Annachi had warned. "The policemen will ask you all sorts of questions and try to see if your answers are satisfactory. They will ask how long have you two been married? Where were you when she hanged herself? Did you two fight often? During any of your fights, did she ever say she was going to kill herself?" Shivan Annachi had also coached him with answers for those questions. An old member of the Congress who was in jail before independence, Shivan Annachi knew the tactics of policemen.

Remembering his first visit to the police station, Veeraiyan wondered if the same cops would still be there. Would they identify him? Again, he thought of Parvathy.

"I should not left Padhinaalu Muri that day. I should not have gone to Alleppey. Hell! I should not have even set up my family in Padhinaalu Muri. Then Parvathy would have been alive." Veeraiyan cursed himself silently.

What a place on earth was Padhinaalu Muri? A place that knew no sunrise or sunset. Everyone lived as they wished. It was supposed to be a community, but there was no sense of one. A place surrounded by cow and buffalo sheds, the stench of dung and hay was familiar to all its residents who had different activities: Cowherds, painters, load carriers, fruit sellers, florists, etc., all working at different places and returning home at night.

Outside every hut was a bench on which the men slept at night. They had no electricity or well for water. Those who slept outside had mosquitoes for company, mosquitoes which never budged and were even immune to the smoke from burning hay. There was a pump on the main road where it curved to Padhinaalu Muri. The Corporation staff did not patrol the place at night, so this was the time for the women of Padhinaalu Muri. They would go there after sunset to bathe, wash clothes, fetch water for the next day, etc.

On the other side of the compound near the cowshed, all sorts of illegal transactions took place at night. With no road lights, the place was dark. There had been gossip of the grass cutter

Chellamma seen with a guy in the dark. If not Chellamma, it was Kaali, else the milkman's wife Govindu. The place was notorious for its unnecessary gossip and wagging tongues at everyone around.

Though her mother had eloped with someone when Parvathy was a kid, she was brought up by her father in a cocoon. He never even sent his daughter to fetch water from the lake or even to the street end, lest someone should comment about her mother. He would go to his store that sold copper and brass utensils, finish business and return home by four in the evening. He would sell his older scrap items at discount to the aluminium shop owner, who would then sell it by weight to the vendor selling dates. This was Reddy's daily routine.

Parvathy, who knew how to make *murukku,* would made a hundred murukkus every night and her father would help by frying them. They would pack and sell them to tea shops by morning. The money earned by selling the murukkus was used to buy rice and oil for next day's murukkus. He would soak the rice in the morning before leaving for work. Parvathy would cook, clean, do her daily chores around the house, then grind the rice into flour and prepare the dough for the murukku. She had her hands full and never had time to indulge in gossip. Her days went by with her dad and murukkus.

"And now I have lost her!" Veeraiyan felt it was his fault that she had died. He couldn't console himself for what had happened. In fact, he had gone to Alleppey only for her sake, else he never had any work at Alleppey. She had wanted to buy a cart with tyres and rent it out in her name to transporters and load carriers for moving goods around the bazaar. Veeraiyan had saved two hundred rupees for the cart. It was at her insistence that Veeraiyan had gone to Alleppey that day.

He was a strong man. When he stood unclothed next to a buffalo, people said they both looked the same. They said he was a Malayali. They also said he was from Sri Lanka. No one knew where he was from. Whichever language he spoke, he sounded like a local. Veeraiyan didn't care. "Oh God!" he thought. "That bastard knew I wasn't going to be home that day."

When Parvathy had come out of their hut to clean the cow dung, he had pounced on her in broad daylight. It was mid-day and all the men had gone to work. It was only the flower seller and the milkman's wife Govindu who were around. Parvathy had cried and shouted for help. But Govindu was just nonchalant and told Parvathy not to cry or wail, to just cooperate with the rapist. Govindu had also slyly pointed out that Parvathy would be following her mother's footsteps.

Grieving for his wife, he recollected, "It was almost two days before I came back from Alleppey, and everything was over by then. Her dad had lost his senses. A post-mortem was conducted on her body. It was Shivan *Annachi* who stood by us. He even offered me a job at his store. She could have waited for me to return. She could have told me what happened before taking her life. I would have killed the man for Parvathy. Now I have no strength to fight. Even if I do, who am I going to fight for? Parvathy, by killing yourself, you have made me a coward. And now I am on my way to the station to tell your story."

The bus came to a halt. Veeraiyan suddenly realized he had missed his bus stop. He got down in a hurry, hoping the conductor wouldn't notice, else he would have to pay the extra fare. He decided to walk back to Paalayam police station.

There was a group of protestors outside the Assembly building, which was on the same road as the police station. They were holding placards and shouting slogans for a strike: "We will not sell our dignity!" "Swallow food! Not our honour!" "Pay us for our work!" They had started the protest at the crack of dawn and the protest had been running for a couple of days.

Veeraiyan pondered over the slogan, "Swallow food! Not our honour!"

He wondered: "What is honour? I left home to save my honour from my father and step-mother. And now Parvathy gave up her life to save her honour."

Just as he entered the police station, the guard outside looked at him. "Are you the case from Padhinaalu Muri? Inspector has been waiting for you."

The guard shouted inside, announcing Veeraiyan's arrival. The inspector looked at him from top to bottom, "Are you the whore's husband? Sign on all these papers. And don't go out of town for a few days without telling us. Do you know to sign your name?" "Sign? For what? Should I sign saying that my wife was a whore? Or should I sign that my wife died to save her honour so that she wouldn't have to hear you call her that?"

—

1. Annachi - A term used to refer to an older male like an elder brother.
2. Padhinaalu Muri - Otherwise called as Fourteenth Bend

PAACHI

Paachi is dead. Life is so uncertain. Naanu had never even imagined that such an event would ever happen. Naanu felt desolate, unable to fathom that his trusted companion Paachi would die and leave him alone suddenly. Life and its very being seemed meaningless.

Bazaar Street was dull. The day was just beginning to dawn. Carts loaded with coconut shells crawled along in a single file like ants. The sound of cart wheels against their axles made a clicking sound that could be heard from afar. None of the shops in the bazaar had opened yet. Only Appu's tea shop had opened. He sprinkled water on the road and the noise of the spoon in the boiler could be heard.

Did anyone in the bazaar know that Paachi had died? Even

if they knew, who would actually care? Naanu couldn't bear it anymore. Even when the folks were returning after watching the late-night movie last night, Paachi was quite active and alive. What could have happened? Naanu couldn't spot a wound from a motor bike or even an insect bite on her body. It was such a shock when he woke up to see Paachi with her tongue hanging out and her eyes rolled up. Her body was stiff and her limbs crooked. She was dead.

Just looking at her body pained Naanu. He couldn't come to terms with her death, couldn't digest his loneliness. Why did she die? Why did she leave him alone? Naanu could only ask these questions but had no answers.

"Hey Naanu? I heard that your Paachi died! I saw her while returning from a night show movie yesterday. I can't believe she is dead. What are you going to do Naanu?" asked Sony.

Naanu looked at Sony, who was wearing khaki shorts that had never seen water, had a *beed*i tucked behind his ear, disheveled hair and stained teeth that had never been brushed. Paachi had never liked Sony. A couple of days back, Sony had barely escaped from Paachi's grip. Had it not been for Naanu, Sony would have been torn to pieces. It was Naanu who had convinced Paachi that Sony was one among them and to just leave him alone.

Sony was far from innocent. As soon as the carts carrying rice sacks lined up outside the godown, Sony went and stood behind the bullocks of a cart and poked the gunny bags to pilfer rice from them. It was Naanu's responsibility to safeguard the rice and if the godown's owner Shankar *Annachi* learnt about the missing rice, it would be Naanu who would have to pay the penalty. So Naanu and

Paachi used to watch the rice like hawks, not letting even a single grain of rice escape. But Sony was a petty thief and Paachi would sniff him out. As soon as Sony poked the gunny bags, Paachi would pounce on him and catch him red-handed. Naanu had to interfere and let him go. Paachi, who was quite intelligent, was indignant to let Sony go.

So when Sony came and conveyed his condolences, Naanu could only sense Sony's relief that now nobody would stop him from pilfering rice and he could live happily by feeding off stolen goods by puncturing sacks stocked in the godown.

The day had dawned fully and pigeons had lined up on the godown roof to feed on the grains spilled from the sacks. Paachi and these pigeons shared an unusual friendship. When the pigeons landed to peck on the grains, Paachi would jump in their midst as if she had found them while playing hide-and-seek. They would get shocked and fly away. Naanu would enjoy watching this game sitting on the bench outside the godown while engrossed in his beedi. Paachi would come back and sit at Naanu's feet with a sense of victory. Naanu would give Paachi a victory pat on her back.

And now that Paachi is dead!

The sun was rising and he could hear the sound of shop shutters being pulled up, people conversing and preparing for daily business. The clock hadn't struck nine yet. Naanu didn't know what to do. He looked at Paachi again. Flies were hovering on her face which gave her a ghostly look. Naanu shooed the flies and covered Paachi's face with a towel. The morning sun shone on her covered face. He lifted her by her legs and moved her to the shade.

Naanu saw Govindan clearing the gutter. All the garbage and rotten fruits and vegetables – tomatoes, cabbage, hay that was used to wrap the vegetables – had clogged the gutter in the market. Govindan used a long rake to clear the gutter which released a stench. Naanu thought it would be better to ask Govindan about the last rites needed for Paachi, since Govindan helped with the last rites for any death that occurred in the slums around the bazaar.

"He would probably give an idea or even help with it. But in return I would have to buy him liquor for the night. Even last month he was the one who took care of the buffalo that had died. He had tied its fore limbs and hind limbs together, loaded it onto a cart and taken it. He skinned it, took its flesh and sold it to the slum folks for a rupee. The horns were sold off for a good price to a shop. What kind of a selfish being is he? To extract a profit out of a dead animal? And what does he do with all the money? He gets drunk and goes to Madhavi's house for the night." thus lamented Naanu with disgust.

"Should I still go and ask him to help with the last rites for Paachi also? What if he skins her and sells her meat as well?" just as Naanu was thinking this, Govindan arrived with his long rake.

"Hey Naanu! I heard that your Paachi has kicked the bucket! She would have died long ago by my spade. She was notorious. So how did she die? Did someone poison her because of their hatred? Or did she get hit by a speeding vehicle? I don't see any wounds on her. I used to hate her so much, but now when I see her body, I feel sad!" Govindan conveyed his condolences to Naanu.

"I'm not sure Govindan. When I woke up this morning she

was gone. Now I need your help in getting her last rites done. Please give me a suggestion." Naanu cut him short so stop his ranting.

"Ok let her remain here. I will clear the gutter till the end of the road and bring my hand cart along. You arrange for my share for the evening. Need to have a cracker of a night." Saying this, Govindan left, pushing his rake along the gutter.

Naanu knew that when Govindan said a cracker of a night, he meant that he needed liquor for the night. Even long after Govindan left, the stench from the gutter lingered. The gong struck nine and business was getting started in the bazaar.

It was Wednesday and Naanu knew that there would not be any carts carrying rice to the godown. Had it been Tuesday or Friday, the streets be choked with carts filled with gunny bags of rice by now, and Paachi would be busy making sure the carts and the rice reached the godown safely. Even the owner of the biggest store who came to the godown before opening his shop had not yet come. Paachi was very lucky to have died today. She died a quiet death.

The sun had risen long ago, but Naanu had not even had tea from the time he woke up. Unable to leave Paachi's corpse unattended, he hadn't even smoked a *beedi*. Naanu wondered if it would even be possible to have such affection towards another human being. Or why is it that human beings don't show such a simple affection towards one another? Paachi had been with him for such a long time as a loyal and faithful friend. They had never been away from each other.

It was only because of her that Naanu even got the job of

guarding the godown at the bazaar, after which he never went hungry even for a day. He also felt responsible, responsible as a human, responsible for another being. She would be by his side day and night and lick the corns on his feet. He was overcome with sorrow on seeing her body now.

All happenings inside the bazaar godown had soon spread to the market area. Kuttappan and Velayudham came running. "Naanu, we heard the news from Govindan. We will take care of the mat and the hay for Paachi's last rites. You don't have to worry." Saying this, they entered the tea shop across the street. Naanu thought they would sit and eat and joke about Paachi with other customers and they all would make fun. Useless fellows! "Wish I could just thrash them," pondered Naanu.

Seeing that there were more flies on Paachi, Naanu shooed them away with his upper garment. It has been a long time since Paachi had come to Naanu. It was the time when Naanu started having corns in his feet and had just bought new footwear. He could hardly move around. If he just sat and guarded the godowns the whole day, the owner would at best give him eight to ten annas, just enough for a meal. With only one garment to wear, it would take him a whole year's work to even buy a change of clothes. When he was younger, fit and able, he could lift sacks on his back the whole day and fill an entire godown. He was earning better then. But with the calluses on his feet, walking itself was painful. Lifting weights became impossible. And that affected his income as well. He went hungry on most days. Word spread and people stopped employing Naanu.

Then one day Naanu spotted Paachi tied to a cart which was

carrying coconuts. Unable to run at the speed of the cart, her legs were being dragged along the road and she was howling in pain. Naanu suspected it to be the work of either Kuttappan or Velayudham. She would have given them a tough fight and to bring her under their control they would have tied her thus. Naanu felt sorry for the poor animal and untied her. He got her tea and food from the tea shop. Paachi gobbled it up hungrily. Since then, both of them had been together. Naanu shared his daily meal with her, talked to her, and at the end of the day when he slept outside the godown, Paachi came and slept next to him. Paachi and Naanu became each other's companion and took care of each other. She started growing and befriended everyone in and around the slum. She got fish and curry from Appu's shop, tea and biscuits from the tea shop, curd rice from someone's house. Paachi was living the life.

Just when things were settling down, a thief entered the godown. It must have been around three or four in the morning. There was a power cut and the streets were pitch dark. The street lights were off and there was not a ray of light. As usual, Naanu was lying on the front porch of the godown. Paachi, who was lying down by his feet, suddenly got up and started barking at the back wall. She came near Naanu, who was sound asleep and barked loudly, then went back to the wall, still barking. She again ran to Naanu and dug the ground with her paws, still barking as if calling out to him. Naanu woke up to the noise and looked in the direction she was indicating, while adjusting his eyes to the darkness.

He got up and stretched himself, thinking of going back to sleep. When Paachi saw Naanu wake up, her barking grew louder. Naanu woke up fully with a jolt and rubbed his eyes. Paachi never barked unnecessarily, and Naanu wondered why she was barking continuously at such an early hour. He wore his slippers and went to have a look.

Behind the wall, a thief had climbed to the top of the godown roof using a drainage pipe, removed tiles and lowered himself into the godown. Naanu immediately went to Appu's tea shop and woke the men sleeping on the porch. He also stopped a few milkmen who were rushing to milk the cattle in the sheds. Gathering all these men because he didn't know how many thieves were inside, he opened the godown and caught the thief red-handed. One of the guys went to the godown owner's house and he came immediately. The police were called.

By the time the case was registered, the rice and missing items accounted for and the thief taken away, it was ten in the morning. The whole street had gathered in front of the godown. Even the town buses which went past the godown slowed down, heard the story and went. It was not every day that people came across thieves and even if they did, he wasn't caught every time.

"Oh there was a thief? Was he caught?" asked a bus driver.

"Yes yes he was caught red-handed!" answered an onlooker.

"Oh who caught him?"

"Oh it's all the work of our Naanu. She resides on the porch of the godown day and night."

"Oh which Naanu? The guy who had corns on his feet and couldn't even walk much? How could he…?"

"Oh didn't you know? He now has a pet Paachi, who found the thief first. Once Naanu spotted the thief there was no escaping." The story spread to the whole town and to nearby towns.

The godown owner was exhilarated. There were goods worth lakhs and lakhs in the godown and the thief who had broken into the godown was caught. The owner was grateful to Naanu and made him permanent caretaker of the godown. He never had to worry about his daily meals anymore.

Naanu was grateful to Paachi since the thief was caught only due to her alertness and warning. She had become the heroine in the area. Wherever she went, she was welcomed with a feast.

When all the shops shut for the day, and all the men had gone home, Paachi would return to the godown porch after feasting at all the places. Naanu would have spread his mat. She would come and curl near his feet. Naanu would smoke his beedi and nod off to sleep while talking to Paachi. Naanu slept well, feeling Paachi's belly rise and fall near him.

Naanu would ask her how her day had been, where she had gone and the items she had feasted on. He would thank her for coming into his life, giving it some meaning and being there for him. Paachi would rub her face on Naanu and wag her tail as if she understood. She would lick his hands and lie next to him. This had become their routine since a long time. It had been so many years since Paachi came into his life that Naanu had lost count.

In this period, ration shops were opened. Kuttappan went off to a big city. Unni, the puny guy, built his body, started lifting weights and became the most sought-after load carrier. Appu employed his brother-in-law in his tea shop who took care of the accounts for a while. Meanwhile, Appu had befriended the local milkmaid Rajamma. A few months later she became pregnant and came to his shop to claim money for their child. She even went on to file a case against him to make him pay for the kid child and her expenses. So much had happened in Bazaar road. The street was dug and laid twice, vehicle movement increased, even buses had started coming into town. All this has happened since Paachi came into Naanu's life.

And now that same Paachi is dead.

Naanu's heart pained to see Paachi lying lifeless. The morning sun was hot. The godown owner came in his car wearing a muslin kurta and dhoti. His driver followed him and opened the big locks of the godown. The owner bent, touched the entrance to the godown and entered.

Naanu realized that the owner didn't know about Paachi's death and wondered how to inform him first thing in the morning. Just at the moment, Govindan brought his cart and parked it near the entrance. Naanu's heart skipped a beat. The cart had a mat that was used to pack food. Flies were hovering on it. All that Naanu could think of was Paachi, who was lying there and that she would be taken away on the cart any minute.

The owner came out after supervising the godown. He saw Govindan with the cart and asked "Hey, how come you are here with your cart? I saw a few rats dead on my way here. You don't need the cart for those rodents."

"No no. It is our Paachi who has died sir. She slept and didn't wake up today. I believe sir hasn't had a chance to see Naanu today." Govindan conveyed the news to the owner. Only then did he turn and look at Naanu, who was standing next to Paachi.

The owner was shocked. "Oh is it our Paachi? What happened? How did she pass away? Was she hit by any lorry or bus? She was such an intelligent animal."

"I don't know sir. She lay next to Naanu last night as usual. When he woke up this morning, she was already dead."

"Is Naanu ok? Is he crying?" was all the owner could ask. He couldn't ask any more questions about the grieving Naanu.

"Govinda, you are taking care of Paachi, right? Make sure you don't just disregard her like you do with other animals. Please dig a grave and make sure she is carefully buried. Poor intelligent dog. She was such a faithful animal. I would say she was even better than all the humans put together in the bazaar. And for you, take this," saying this, the owner gave him five rupees.

Naanu felt sick inside. It was as if someone had removed his footwear and made him walk on hot cement with his feet full of calluses. "This is it. Govindan is going to take her away any moment now. Paachi is going to leave me forever…" he cried to himself.

"I don't have anyone anymore. My mom eloped with a mason when I was a kid, my father was killed in a street fight… Sold grass in the slums until I was eighteen, washed buffaloes and did all odd jobs. Came to the bazaar, became a labourer and stayed here. Developed corns on both feet and became dependent on the godown and its porch. Paachi came into my life and gave it some meaning. Now she's gone, and with her everything is gone. She will be taken away and with that, everything will be over." Naanu was overcome with emotions.

"Naanu I'm going to take her now. Do you have any last rites?" asked Govindan. Naanu just stood there, not knowing or feeling anything.

"Ok I can understand that you are mourning. I will take care," saying this, Govindan lifted Paachi and placed her on the cart. Naanu looked at her one last time. Her mouth was open and all her pearly white teeth shone under the sun. Her legs were spread across. She looked just like she slept next to him every night.

Govindan pulled the cart and went on his way. The godown owner came and consoled Naanu once. The car driver looked at Naanu from inside the car.

Paachi is dead, leaving Naanu alone and desolate. The sun continues to rise high.

—

Carpe Diem

Appukuttan was lost in thought as he sat on the bench with a broken blade, cutting the corns off his feet. He cursed Velappan under his breath.

It was just two days back when Velappan had sarcastically said, "Appukutta! You have the knack of making even the most intelligent folks fall for your gimmicks!" Since that day, it had been a struggle to earn enough even for a square meal. The last two days had passed by without much fanfare. Today being Monday, Appukuttan was hoping for a positive start to the week. Sitting with his feet on the bench, he thought, "What has gotten into people's minds today? How come not even one person has shown his face? These people normally come in hordes to watch me say 'Can you see the white pig fly?' and believe it. But today, not a soul is to be seen!!" It was just a while since the day had begun and the shops in the bazaar had opened. He was hoping for a stroke of luck soon.

Just then, a loud siren broke the silence, signaling the beginning of a harthal (strike) for the day. A union minister had been killed and the party cadre had called for a strike, asking all shops to be shut down. Not knowing what to do with his stock of freshly made products, the owner of a corner tea shop decided to keep it open. Unfortunately for him, people from the party demolished the furniture and brought the shop down within seconds.

With all the shops on Bazaar road shut down to avoid any damage to their property, the whole stretch wore a deserted look. The harthal seemed to stretch Appukuttan's bad luck further; every time he felt a pang of hunger, he cursed Velappan for his statement. Seeing a man walk past, he and asked for the time. "Half past eleven" was the answer. He realized almost half the day was over and it was time for lunch. Telling himself that he could not afford to sit like this for long, he threw the blade, got up and wore his slippers. He decided to take a walk… But where would he go?

He looked towards the east. Nothing but emptiness. He turned west. He could only see the line of shut shops stretching till the horizon. Deserted street, scorching heat and the mirage that gave a molten lava feel. It was hard to see such an empty street, especially on the first Monday of the month. But that was the reality of a strike in Kerala.

He decided to look around to take note of his surroundings. The electric wires overhead had crows here and there. The huge garbage bin near the florist had a couple of boys inside it, scavenging for whatever they could find useful. A street dog just ran across to find some shelter and escape the heat. He could just see some empty pull carts here and there without their owners. Just then, a fully loaded covered lorry sped past, raising a thick cloud of dust. As the lorry could not unload the stock due to the strike, the driver decided not to stop and create unnecessary problems or lose his stock. Appukuttan covered his face with his shoulder cloth and walked towards the west. Some shopkeepers who couldn't open their shops were sitting outside in a group and talking. A couple of them were reading a newspaper. He walked on. A few shopkeepers were returning home with no hope of opening shop for the day.

Appukuttan realized that all these people were locals, none was from out of town, so he could not scam any of them, and moved on.

He wondered if he had forgotten the tricks of his trade, not having been able to put it to test over the last two days. He decided to run it in his mind as he walked the deserted streets.

He visualized a guy holding bronze vessels tied in palm leaves on his head. He looked like someone with the words 'Take my money' written all over him. Appukuttan would go to him with the face of a lost child and start talking to him. "Aren't you Kunjipillai from Poojapura? How are you? It's been so long since I saw you last," as if they were old acquaintances. This man would get stumped at this sudden conversation by a total stranger and looked around to see if the question was directed at him.

Appukuttan would continue. "Brother Kunjipillai seems to have forgotten me. Yeah, must have been six to eight years since I last saw him. That's why he has forgotten me."

The stranger had no recollection of seeing Appukuttan and said "Oh no! You must have confused me with someone. I am not from Poojapura. I am from Kundaambaagam."

Appukuttan, having decided not to let go of this guy, would continue. "Oh! Where in Kundaambaagam?"

If the stranger asked, "Where exactly in Kundaambaagam are

you from or who do you know there?" Appukuttan would respond with, "My native place is just off Kundaambaagam, in a place called Valiaveedu. Do you know Kochunni? (a common name in parts of Kerala and every village has more than a couple of guys with this name)"

"Sorry, I don't know any Kochunni. I guess you have mistaken me with someone else. I have to catch a bus back home." Just before this guy moved, Appukuttan would deliver his closing response. "Oh! I am sorry. I guess I really have mistaken you with someone else. Well I thought I could just ask you for a small favour. I came to the bazaar for some urgent work and am heading back home. But I just realized that I am short of 50 paise for the bus fare. I feel bad to ask you, but I cannot ask anyone else. Seeing that we are both from the same place, it would be great if you could help me out of this fix."

This man would hurriedly search his pockets and with a sly smile give some change, take leave and depart. This was the manner in which Appukuttan earned his daily bread.

There were so many types of gullible people in the world, yet Appukuttan couldn't meet even one such person today. With this thought, he walked along the street of Sabapathy temple, turned east of Vaaniyankulam road onto Power House Street and crossed Shakthi Theatre. It was a forced holiday due to harthal and the roads were almost deserted, except for a couple of folks here and there. The whole town bore a sad cursed look that made this day seem even hotter than usual.

Just outside Shakthi theatre, on this hot day, there was a gang of scammers playing cards and fleecing an innocent guy who was their scapegoat for the day. When a person who had lost all his money asked them for at least some change, their reply would be, "You came and lost all your money. Now run before we beat you up."

"People like these scammers who loot people off every little penny will get scapegoats, but others like me who just want a solid meal will never find a single customer," despaired Appukuttan, who was getting frustrated and losing energy. Slowly he climbed the stairs of the over-bridge. A blind beggar was sitting on the steps with a towel and some scattered coins. Appukuttan though it was better to be a beggar where money just falls on your plate. Even if you don't earn on a particular day, there is no loss.

He climbed down the stairs of the bridge. Via Sri Kumar theatre, he walked towards Thambanoor bus stand and railway station, and crossed a park. He looked inside and saw a beggar sleeping under the board "Beggars not allowed."

Appukuttan walked the entire town on an empty stomach, in the scorching heat and started feeling dejected about life. Hunger was eroding his stomach. He started feeling dizzy. He drank the road-side tap water to satiate his hunger until he couldn't drink any more. He was no stranger to hunger; still, the thought that he would not be able to get food today was unbearable. He felt sorry for himself.

He promised himself that he would not fleece people, but would make an honest living henceforth. Deciding to sell goods from a shipyard or even peanuts for a living, he promised himself that he would mend his ways and live an honest life.

Such thoughts came unbidden to Appukuttan whenever hunger pangs bit him. These thoughts remained only until the next morning and evaporated when he met an innocent scapegoat, and until such time that the scapegoat's money came into Appukuttan's hands. He would then opine, "When I can get such easy money, why would I slog in a shipyard? And even after I slog, the income would not be much. Let's see when it happens," and go looking for the next scapegoat to fleece, or go to spend his ill-gotten money.

But today was not such a day. After walking the whole day on an empty stomach, he could feel the walls of his stomach sticking together. Before it got dark, Appukuttan wanted to find a place to rest his tired feet. He walked on Arya Road, turned east, took his earlier route, then turned left towards the Tamil school. Luckily for him, the school's tin gate was open. Just near the school courtyard, he found a cement bench outside a classroom. Darkness had begun to set in and he couldn't think much. He went inside the school, took his shoulder towel, dusted the bench, then spread the towel and lay down on it.

The empty stomach, tired body from all the walking and dejected mind didn't allow him to sleep immediately. He didn't have much to think about. No family, no house, no work to be completed. Hence he had very little to think about other than his growling stomach that needed to be fed. He looked up at the sky and saw the scattered stars.

Beyond the school compound wall, he could see the dark outlines of coconut trees. Nearby was a buffalo shed, from which came the stench of animal waste. The situation was well suited for the swarm of mosquitoes that started singing near his ears. Slowly, Appukuttan drifted off to sleep.

Suddenly, a group of men were causing a commotion beyond the school compound wall, hitting and swearing at each other. This sudden ruckus woke Appukuttan. He felt someone sitting at his feet and jumped up with a start. He could see the figure of a lady seated by his feet in the dark. She smelt of dried flowers.

To make things clear, he asked, "Are you a woman?"

"Shhhhh.... Talk softly!" She replied in a hushed tone. "Who are you? The watchman of this school? You were snoring so loudly here. Did that sound wake you up?" She asked, pointing her finger in the direction of the noise.

"The men who brought me here are fighting and arguing among themselves as to who should have me first. Guess they will come only after they decide who the winner is, or once one of them beats the others."

She spoke very openly about herself. Even before he could get over his fear, Appukuttan understood who she was and the situation at hand.

She pulled out a beedi and asked, "Do you have a light, Mr. Watchman?"

"I don't have a light or anything on me. Who are you?" asked Appukuttan in irritation.

"Who? Me? I don't have an address to call my own. I am care of platform. Ok, now see this. Can you see?" Saying this, she pulled out some notes and said, "Twenty two rupees! Those man gave it to me as an advance for my services. Do you know who they are? They are the scammers. God knows which innocent guy lost his earnings to them today. It has landed in my hands. They brought me here so that they can comfortably have me here. Do they know that you are here?"

Appukuttan, very irritated after the previous day's fiasco, got up, took his towel, and grumbled, "You guys have this place. I will go to that dark place over there. Finish your work soon and leave." Saying this, Appukuttan mumbled something to himself and started walking away from her.

This woman called him "Mr. Watchman! I need a small favour from you! Can you keep this twenty two rupees with you? They will finish their work with me and fleece me of this money. I can't fight them. Just don't make much noise in the dark. I shall take care of you later." Saying this, she handed the money over to Appukuttan.

Appukuttan took the money from her. He recollected that while he was walking along Shakthi theatre in the scorching heat, he had seen some persons swindling an innocent man and he replayed the scene in his mind. What was lost there was now in his hands. Just then she said, "Please wait near that street, Mr. Watchman," in a hushed tone. Just as Appukuttan was leaving, one guy jumped over the school gate and came inside hurriedly.

He called out to the lady, "Come, come, let's get going before someone else tries to make out with you!" Appukuttan couldn't hear what she replied. His brain started working in overdrive. He used the pitch darkness in the school to his benefit. He found a place where the wall was broken near the buffalo shed and jumped out through the gap. He stepped on cow dung, but it didn't matter. He walked out onto the street and the lights were as bright as day. Appukuttan was richer by twenty-two rupees now.

He thought of the chain of actions. The scammers snatched the money from an innocent man on the road. They gave the money to this prostitute for their pleasure. She trusted the school's watchman and gave the money to him.

Appukuttan felt the money in his pocket and walked in the brightly lit street with a big smile. "I am not Mr. Watchman. I am Appukuttan." He had seized the opportunity.

The Eighth Day

"**P**athaaaan…"

"Hey Pathan!"

"Get lost, you useless fellows…"

The boys from the neighborhood are making fun of Pathan and his misshapen swollen hand. Looking like an elephant trunk that has no bone, it weighs him down. The boys scatter and run like a flock of birds when a stone thrown in their middle.

"I will crush you all like peanuts." Saying this, Pathan tries to slap them. His hand falls on the thatched walls like a sloth. "Aaaaah!" he groans as the pain is unbearable.

Pathan woke up startled…

"Just a dream. Phew! These boys taunt me even in my sleep."

The sun was scorching outside. Pathan couldn't open his eyes. He had developed some eye infection that made it difficult for him to see the bright sun. Pathan was not bothered about the eye problem, but it was the doctor at the clinic whose words had stung the most.

"What did you do all these days? Did you wait for it to get rotten before coming to see me? It is already beyond repair. If the infection spreads from your hand to your brain, there is no way to save you. Starting today, come here for a daily injection for eight days. After that, I will refer you to the medical college hospital. They will decide whether your hand has to be amputated or not. I don't have hope… I feel your hand has to be amputated below your elbow. This would not have happened had you been careful from the beginning. As I said, come here and take an injection daily for the next eight days. We shall see later…"

Pathan started talking to himself…

Cutting off hands and legs seems to be a simple thing for the doctor, just like cutting grass. I would not be surprised if he even chopped off my head one day and asked me to walk. If I don't have my hand, I would never be able to walk freely on Bazaar Road in front of these boys. Not even a stray dog will respect me if I have only one hand.

Now every guy whose name is Pathan thinks he is me. Not everyone can be me. They cannot do everything that I have done. It is not fair. Crazy fellows. If only I could get rid of my drinking habit. Nowadays, even a small drink of six ounces makes my legs wobble at the knees and my mouth starts blabbering on its own. The bazaar boys take advantage of that and start mocking me.

When these boys start mocking, I am unable to chase them, so I resort to abusing them. This becomes a comic act for the onlookers and the boys have their share of fun. As much as I try, when the boys start talking two words, I must retort with four words, else I am unable to sleep that night.

No matter what happens, I should never let the doctor chop my hand. It is just eight days. I shall go to the bazaar doctor and take the injections. I will cut down on my alcohol and eating fried food. That should speed the process and help in the healing. It is suffocating to stay indoors in this hut. The heat and the stench nearby are making it unbearable.

The slum has seen a makeover in the last few years and has become a colony. A pipe brings water into the houses. The swampy areas have been filled with soil and trees have been planted around. Coconut trees are abundant. If only the Corporation takes notice and builds toilets instead of the inhabitants having to defecate in the open, the colony will be complete.

The colony and its residents are all I know in the last five or six years. What to do? My limbs have given up on me. Every day is not the same. Age has caught up. I was almost fifteen when I came to this slum near the bazaar. Now I have crossed fifty. I am unable to flex or lift my hands… Even if I stay indoors the whole day, I am neither able to turn and lie nor sleep in the same position. My eyes feel as if a thousand needles are piercing through them, making it difficult to open them.

—

"Pathan... Pathan… are you inside? Are you sleeping? How is

your eye infection? Don't keep lying down the whole day. Get up and splash cold water in your eyes repeatedly. Put the eye drops that the doctor had given. How is your hand? Is there any improvement after your visit to the doctor? Are you able to flex your hand…?" It was Govindan, the gutter cleaner.

A dark round guy, Govindan resembled a worm digging through the earth: Reddish eyes, oval face, muscular limbs, broad chest, and khaki shorts with a vest. He was a pest but very good at heart. He had come to see Pathan after finishing his morning routine. Govindan lived life king-size. He started his work at seven in the morning. With his rake, he would start at Elavaaniya Street till the junction at Sannadhi Street, then from Sannadhi junction to Sabapathy Temple. He would clear the gutters on both sides of the street and dump the garbage on the same sides of the street. By ten, he would go to the sanitary office to return the rake to the overseer. The shopkeepers paid ten to fifteen paisa so that Govindan would take care not to dump the garbage in front of their shops. He also received a salary. Of course he lived his life king-size…

"Come in Govindan. Things have not been the same ever since I came back from the doctor. I don't know the very purpose of my life. I have to go to the doctor for eight days. What if they decide to amputate my hand? Think about it Govindan… Think about the life I lived. Already these kids in Bazaar Street don't respect me or consider me for anything. If my hand is chopped and I become a handicapped…" Pathan's voice quivered.

Seeing that Pathan was almost crying, Govindan consoled him. "You know those boys. Why do you keep talking back to them? Only because you talk back to them, they keep making fun. Just act deaf and ignore them. They will also just go quietly."

"I am not used to being quiet Govindan. Think of the life I have lived here. There was no one else who was as bold as me in Bazaar Street. You think kids like these would have the courage to come and stand in front of me and speak to me few years back? Now on the pretext of calling someone else, they just shout 'Pathan' loud enough for me to hear. How do you expect me to keep quiet, Govindan?"

"Don't worry about all that and lie down. It's only eight days. Go to the doctor without fail every day and take your injections. The swelling and the infection in your hand will reduce, so calm down and rest…"

"But the doctor didn't say it like that Govindan, I think I might have to lose my hand. I don't have much hope. I have behaved so arrogantly and done the nastiest of things with this hand. The doctor knows all that I have done. He will definitely chop off my hand…"

"I don't think the doctor would have meant it. He would have said it so that you will be careful henceforth. All those are tricks doctors use on patients. Don't lose hope. Did you drink the porridge I gave? Looks like you didn't…"

"Govinda, the porridge that you gave me is in the same place. I don't feel like having anything. Can you please get me six ounces of alcohol from Narayanan's shop? I used to drink by the pitcher. Now I can't go beyond six ounces. I have money on the shelf."

"Pathan, even in this stage you can only think of alcohol, is it? Apply some spicy chillies on your tongue and don't even think of alcohol for the next eight days. Just stay calm. Your hand is ripe with infection. Whether you die or not, at least have a peaceful and painless death. Drink the porridge I brought, wash your face and put the medicine in your eyes. It's two in the afternoon and I have some work at the sanitary office. Just lie down and don't think of anything. Don't even think of walking all the way to the liquor shop. In case you want something to drink, my son will be at the tea shop. He will get something for you."

Pathan watched as Govindan walked and crossed the widest gutter in the slum until he disappeared.

It was a straight line from Pathan's hut to Ilavaaniya Amman's temple junction. The temple was on the middle of the road, which took a southern turn and joined Sannadhi Road junction, which led to the bazaar. The other road turned east and went into the fish market, the palm sugar store and the vegetable shop that sold produce from the mountains. The street beyond the temple went north towards Manakaadu.

What was there in Manakaadu? All the tenements of Nairs who had settled on the marsh land of the historical Thiruvidhankoor temple along with the bazaar and the Kali Temple. The colony was between the bazaar and Manakaadu. Most of this colony's residents were labourers working for the Corporation. Amongst them lived the bazaar's load bearers and Pathan. At the eastern end of the colony was the long cement sewage pipe that drained out the waste water from the whole city into the sea. The small thatched boxes alongside the pipe were all houses. On the other side of the sewage pipe stood a lone cottage made of bamboo leaves, which belonged to Natarajan, the local brewer. Natarajan's hut stood like a jeweled crown for the whole colony. It was a big boon, not only to the colony's residents, but even for the shop owners in the bazaar.

Having been sick and indoors the whole day, Pathan felt like walking up to Natarajan's store for a drink. But he could not. Not only Govindan, if anyone else from the colony saw him in this state, they would definitely object to Pathan drinking. Govindan's wife Paachi or Sellappan would never allow him to leave the house. They were such loyal folks.

Pathan couldn't open his eyes to look out. His eyes were irritated as if sand had been poured on his face. As if this wasn't enough, his hand was swollen so much that it looked like an infant was lying next to him. His hand had been lying motionless for such a long time that Pathan had lost all sensation in his limb. Did he feel no pain in his hand because of the medicines, he wondered. His mouth was dry, he didn't feel hungry at all. Pathan had drunk tea before going to the hospital that morning. That was the last thing that had touched his lips. Govindan's wife had left porridge in the pot, which remained untouched.

Pathan's eyes felt heavy and drowsy. Towards the north, he could hear children play in the coconut grove. Beyond the coconut grove in the cinema theatre, a new movie must have been released. A song being played in the matinee show was faintly audible. Had it been late into the night, the song would have sounded loud and boisterous. He could hear what seemed like Govindan's son's voice along with the voices of other kids of the neighbourhood.

Pathan was overwhelmed with emotions and his eyes welled up. He closed his mouth and cried. After a while, he wiped the tears with his left hand. Using the towel covering his torso, he covered his mouth so that the sound of his crying could not be heard outside. He swallowed and looked outside. The streets wore a deserted look, which only made him more emotional. Again, he started thinking aloud...

If only we stayed young forever, life would be so pleasant. We could just roam freely, without a worry in the world. Only the weak hearted cry for everything. But how is it fair to say that I am weak hearted? No one in this colony or even in this city would have dared to do half the things that this Pathan would have done. To think of the illustrious life I lived, and to compare it with my life now… It is unbearable. I have never had anyone, no father or mother, no wife or children. No one to call my own…

Govindan has advised me innumerable times, "Get married to some woman, don't worry about caste or age or anything. It is important to have someone to call your own. If you ever fall sick, you need someone to give you water or make sure you are ok. Your friends or neighbours will not come running to you forever. Even I will not come and see you always. We have drunk together, you have fed me many times, and yes, we are good friends. But when you fall sick, I can only take care of you for a while. All that will last only for a while, after which things will go sour. You had deposited your money with me long ago, which is why I am tending to you and feeding you. You are not that old yet. Find a girl and marry her, she will be with you till the end. You never know. Your girl might be here in the colony itself."

Why was it that every time there was talk of marrying a girl, my thoughts flew back to the past? I think I will take these thoughts to my grave. If I do find a girl, she has to be one who enjoys life as she did. Even if she is going to live with me till the end, she has to be like that girl. If I had to find someone in this colony, I would have found her long ago. After that I have seen so many broads. Not even one can come close to her. But if someone were to ask me today what kind of a girl she was, what did she look like, I would not know. I didn't see her face. It all happened on one night, on a rainy night. I didn't bother about my demeanour or any decorum. Thinking about that night still gives me goose bumps. Something that I can't forget so easily.

It would have been twenty-five years ago. Or more? I would have been around nineteen or twenty years old then. It was the year after the Killi river got flooded, around the Gemini month. In those days the colony and the bazaar wore a different look. From the fort on the eastern end till Arya street, for half-a-mile, both sides of the street were filled with low-raised shops. There was no shop that did not have a tiled roof and oil lantern in front. There were no electric lamps to be seen anywhere. Every street had a kerosene lamp. There were some shops on Kothuvaal Street and Sabapathy Temple Street that had gas lamps as well.

At the end of Sannadhi Street was a green post box with a conch painted on it. It was Raja Moolam Thirunal's reign at that time. He had renounced his throne and in his place Amma Rani was ruling. I had seen Amma Rani once, only once, when she passed by the bazaar for the prayers…

That was the period when the fathers and grandfathers of the traders from the Chettiyar family had their business, both wholesale and retail. I used to work there carrying loads, bringing the goods from the bazaar, delivering goods to households in the beginning of each month – goods like rice, bronze ware to the households who bought on a regular basis. That was my main job in the bazaar.

That was when I had seen Trivandrum fully and knew the streets, lanes and by lanes, so that I could avoid the crowded main roads.

Thambanoor Bus Stand, Railway Station, the junction of Palayam General Hospital, Buddha Market, Sastha Mangalam, the place which had the king's shed, the big market of the town, the empty lands, the shops and all the other landmarks were as familiar as drinking water.

As a load carrier, it was easy to earn twenty or twenty-five *chakkaram* on a daily basis those days. It was not like today, when money is calculated as annas and paise. *Chakkaram*, rupee and half rupee were the coins with the Maharaja's conch and flower symbol. There was also the smallest one pie. One c*hakkaram* equals sixteen coins, four c*hakkarams* equaled one silver rupee, seven rupees equaled twenty-eight Chakkaram and one rupee. This was the calculation. The chakkaram of that day is equal to a rupee of today. For three chakkaram, one could get a good quantity of Samba rice. In Sadhu's tea shop, one could eat pudding for eight pies or half a chakkaram. No one used to eat only one pudding. The aroma from the dosai and sambar at the tea stall wafts through my nose even today…

It was a Tuesday as far as my memory goes. As soon as the sun set, it started raining heavily. From Sannadhi Junction to Elavaaniya Street, it was flooded and the water rose to knee level. The vegetable market street, the walls, the whole town was flooded. It was the first week of the month and a busy time for business, and more than half the businessmen in the town would buy retail stocks from the Pathan Chettiyar's shop. As soon as a new month began, all the small shop owners would bring bronze vessels to be filled with rice and lists as long as their arms.

They would give the money and the lists, and it was I who delivered their monthly groceries to each of their houses. I knew all the important men who worked in Hajur Hospital. They all adored me. The reason was that I never bargained with them for my charges. Even if they paid me a meagre eight paise, I used to take it without arguing. If I went to some houses during their mid-day meal, I used to get fed too.

Since it was raining that day, all the folks handed over their lists to Chettiyar and went home early. I sat at the porch of the shop, curled up in a corner. That was when my boss the Chettiyar called me and asked me to make a delivery to the house up the hill.

"Hey Pathan! There is a delivery to be done to the house up the hill. It is all packed and bundled up. The sun has set. If we keep looking at the rain, nothing will happen. Put a mat on top of the bundle to protect it from the rain, go and deliver it and quickly come back."

"Where is the house boss?" I asked him

"House? Didn't you hear what I just said? Don't you know the house up the hill with walls high up like a fort? It is near the shed, go and ask for the house up the hill, anyone will guide you. There will be a guard at the entrance."

"Alright boss... What about my wages?"

"They will pay you there. Take whatever they give and don't argue or bargain with them. In case it is less I shall pay you the remaining amount. In case it is in excess you take it. Sometimes they might even pay you in silver if they don't have change. Go and deliver the goods without thinking too much."

The desire created by Chettiyar boss, along with the frustration of having to sit in the same place in the rain, gave me the motivation to leave immediately.

With a turban on my head, as soon as I entered the fort, the bell at Pappanaswamy temple rang eight times. With the rain drizzling and no clothing on my torso, I felt chill. In those days, men didn't wear anything above the waist, just a dhoti and turban. It was pitch dark outside. The small oil lanterns placed at equal intervals emitted a little light through their glass cases, but hardly anything was visible outside in the rain. On the banks of the Padmatheertha pond, someone was washing clothes even at that time in that heavy rain. There was some light from the shops on the bank of the pond. On crossing the pond and turning into the street, again it was pitch dark.

I was carefully choosing my steps in the rain water and walking with the load on my head. Whenever it rains, all the load carrying boys sing a song composed by them and apt for the situation. It goes like this…

Rain drops drizzling
Hot Sugar Beets steaming,
With just a thin saree for Cover
My dear Paru is waiting

For boys of age seventeen to eighteen years, their thoughts wander haywire. I walked the entire route inquiring along the way, and didn't notice how far I had come. But once I neared the house, I didn't ask anyone… That was not because there was not a soul in sight. I could have asked in any of the small shops nearby. I turned to a shop with my turban and the load, lit a *beedi* on the burning rope. I wanted to see if I could find my way in Thiruvananthapuram without asking anyone.

As I walked further, I found a house where a guard stood outside on my own. As soon as I saw the guard outside, the row of lights leading up to the house, then the house itself, I realized that I had reached my destination. At the entrance, wearing a helmet and a coat even in the heavy rain, the guard looked like an Englishman. When I showed him the bill from Pathan Chettiyar's shop and the load on my head, he let me in without question.

Well-built houses with tiled roofs and courtyards with lanterns lined the street. The rain water in the courtyard displayed colourful patterns from the lantern light – there was no one outside. I lowered the load from my head to the patio, removed the turban from my head and used it to wipe my body. I peeped inside the house. I could see some light coming through the window from inside. The windows and door had a light green curtain that did not allow light to escape out – but the inside of the house looked as beautiful as a cinema hall. It glittered beautifully in the faint light and the smell was that of a perfume.

"Madam, madam, anybody home?" I called out. When addressing the lady of the house in big houses like this, the lady of the house has to be addressed as 'Madam'. There was no sound even after some time. I called out again. The courtyard looked scary. There was a huge shed beyond the wall, and then a small forest with lots of flowers and shrubs. From there one could get the fragrance of peaches along with the smell of the rain-drenched soil. The trees stood tall in the dark and in the rain. The temple tower beyond could be seen only during the day. Nothing else was visible in the rainy night.

"Who is that standing in the courtyard?"

The soft and sweet voice of a woman was heard. Still no light.

"I am coming from Chettiyar's provision store and I have brought groceries." I respectfully conveyed the reason for my visit.

"Groceries? Why has it taken so long? Bring the load from the courtyard."

I groped my way in the dark, took the load and went to the entrance on the northern end. A door opened and allowed some light in. Still the path was very dark.

"Keep the things inside the store room. I had lit the wall light inside, but it looks like the wind has extinguished it. Keep the things along the wall inside the store room."

The woman with the sweet voice stood between the dark northern room and the lit room. The instant I kept the load on the floor of the store room, the rain that was drizzling till then started pouring heavily. I stood inside the store room with the groceries near my feet. The rain was getting heavier by the second. The room had a somewhat pleasant mixed smell of camphor, oil, dried coconut, sugar, jaggery and rotten bananas. It was the store room of a big house. I thought of the elaborate meals and desserts that followed after lunch every day. They would have had *kheer* with *papadum* every day.

"Hey you guy from Chettiyar's shop. It is raining very heavily. Are you scared to go back at night?"

The same woman – she was asking if I was afraid of the dark. Her voice sounded like she was near. There was an oil lamp flickering in a nearby room. Still I was not able to see the person whose voice I had been hearing. Had I known what was going to happen next, I would have made all efforts in trying to see the face to whom the voice belonged. At that time, all I that I could think was – the rain should stop for some time, I should reach the store before the boss shuts shop. If she gives me the money, I will leave even if it is drizzling. I felt embarrassed to be standing in that awkward place for so long. From her voice, I felt that the woman could be a young lady of the household. It would be disrespectful of me to peep outside to see her face, so I just stood there in the store room, freezing in the cold.

As I stood there, I found a vessel and leaned on it for support. The cold, the warmth of the vessel, the rain outside and the darkness, I dozed off.

Rain drops drizzling
Hot Sugar Beets steaming,
With just a thin saree for Cover
My dear Paru is waiting

I am not sure if I had fainted or dozed off. I am not sure how long it was before I woke up. I felt some movement near me, stealthy as a cat. I felt someone's hand on my chest. Who was it? I woke up startled, not sure if it was a dream. It was dark. It smelt like the store room. I realized someone had bent down towards me.

"You are the man from Chettiyar's shop, right?"

It was that woman's voice. She came and whispered near my ear…

I was still in a daze, frightened and cold, I could not think clearly. It was still drizzling and there was a cold wind blowing…

"Don't worry…"

The woman's hand felt the length of my hand, pulled it and kept it on her breasts. Her hand felt as soft as cotton... When my hand touched her body, every hair on my body was standing on end. I was sweating in spite of the cold. I didn't know what it was. She took my right hand. Caressed it. Kissed it.

"Why does your hand have so many calluses?" she asked.

"It is because of all the loads I carry…" I tried to speak, but words failed me. I was half in fear, half in shock.

"What is your name?" she asked.

"Syed Pathan."

"Oh, you are a Pathan by caste is it? Are you fair or dark?"

"I am dark."

"Dark? I did not know that there were dark people among Pathans. I have seen fair Pathans. The guys who rear the horses are all fair Pathans."

"I do not know about that. I am dark!"

"It doesn't matter. How does it matter in the dark?"

Then she hugged me tight. That is all I can remember. Even the very thought of it sends waves of shivers even now.

She woke me before dawn. It was like asking someone to get up half way through a wedding feast! She gave me seven rupees and a silver coin. She asked me to leave without letting the guard outside see me. She begged me not to tell anyone about whatever had happened during the night…

When I got down and walked down the streets, it had stopped raining. The road was wet from the rain. The wind was chill, the trees on both side of the street swayed in the wind. The temple clock rang a few times, but the time did not register in my head. It appeared to be almost sunrise. The night, the rain, the thrill of the previous night. A thrill I had not experienced until then. I did not get another night like that until now. Neither did I get someone like that to spend the night with.

After that night, whenever I went to the temple or by the fort, I used to look at the house... The guard stood outside. Inside the gate stood a jackfruit tree with fruits hanging from it. The elephant shed and the caretakers could be seen. But I never saw any one. After that, I went to drop goods to that house a couple of times. The cook would come and take the goods to the store room. But the woman I searched for was never seen again.

Over time, I started longing for her. Slowly the yearning became an obsession. If I am going to be with someone, it should be with someone like her, else I never felt the need for any woman or any other comfort. Twice a year, when the Maharaja came out to the streets for the chariot festival, his procession came through that route to reach the sea. I would go there to see if I could spot the woman who had been with me that night. All the women of the house would come out and stand at the entrance of the house. Who among them would it be? The one who was with me during the rainy night!

Definitely it had to be one of the ladies of the house! Not a servant or an old lady. The smell that emanated from her could definitely not come from a lady who swept the house or from a cook or any other maid of the house. It was such a divine smell! Maybe she would be able to recognize me if she saw me…

Two years after that incident, I left Chettiyar's shop. After that, I didn't take groceries to any houses. Somehow, time has flown all these years.

—

A sudden loud noise brought Pathan back to his senses. He saw that a gang of four or five policemen were chasing someone inside the colony. All the men, women and children ran behind them to see the drama that would unfold. Outside the slum on Elavaaniya Street, a gang of men stood and gaped at the police chasing and beating thieves.

The day was coming to an end. "Was I lying down all this while, without realizing the day pass by?" Pathan was surprised by how quickly time flew by. To him, the time seemed the same as in the morning. The stinging pain in his eyes had reduced considerably. Using his left hand, he wiped his right eye and saw that the yellow sun was between the coconut trees. The heat was unbearable. Chakkiliyan, who had recently taken residence in the colony, had set up a stove at the base of the coconut tree and was boiling porridge. No matter how much wood he got, he always used only rubber to light a fire. "Useless fellow," Syed Pathan cursed under his breath, feeling hungry.

Sitting in his hut, he leaned slightly to see through the hole. Looking around, as far as his eye could see, Pathan could not see a single soul. All of them had gone behind the policemen to see what was happening in the south. He suspected it would be Natarajan from the liquor shop who had been arrested. Chakkiliyan's toddler and young daughter were the only beings near the stove at the base of the coconut tree. "I felt like having like having tea, and looked for Govindan's son Kuttan, but even he cannot be seen," thought Pathan. He leaned on his left hand and slowly got up from his bed. He took a beedi from the shelf and lit it with his left hand. All his functions with only one hand… Smoking his beedi, Pathan came out from his hut and thought, "I have to slowly walk and make my way to Appu's tea shop." He pulled and shut the door to his hut, crossed the stream and stepped onto the streets.

"Hey Pathan is coming, Pathan is coming…"

"Let him come, that motherfucker. I will handle him today."

"Leave him. Of late he has not been keeping well and has been visiting the community doctor. His right hand has been put in a sling and is suspended from his neck. Did you see?"

"Yes, that pesky guy should get more than this. He has not done anything good with those hands. Now he is cradling and singing lullabies to his hands. Is he coming this side? Wait, let me collect stones to welcome him."

Syed Pathan crossed Sannadhi junction and walked on. It was around ten or eleven in the morning with the sun shining down. There were shops selling perfumes, sandal paste, etc. on both sides of the street. There were Muslim stores that had arranged betel leaves in a conical tower shape, with betel nuts grouped in front of them… Beyond the shops, what was once a Sadhu's hut, now belonged to Appu and his tea shop.

This hut now had two portions, with the bottom portion for

labourers and others to drink tea on wooden benches and tables. The top portion was for those who came wearing white shirts and turbans to have their tiffin. After this was the provision store, tobacco shops, traditional medicine shops, stores that sold ropes, moneylender's shop, and mostly small business shops. It was peak business time. He ignored the jibes from the slum boys and kept walking.

Pathan was quite tall, maybe six feet or more. Dark complexion. Looking at him, one could not decide how old he would be – around forty-five or fifty years old. He wore a lungi. His hand was supported by a towel from his neck. His eyes looked droopy as if he was woken up from sleep, graying hair that stood erect, flat nose, Rajendra Prasad type of moustache; if his hand was left loose from its support, it would look like an elephant's trunk. His left hand appeared normal. What if he had elephantiasis? Being right-handed, he felt comfortable using his right hand. "Don't play with Pathan. If he lifts his huge right hand and strikes you, it is instant death," was a prevalent rumour. When Pathan had been hale and healthy, the boys in the street used to vanish like flies at his sight. Now that Pathan was frail and weak, the boys were teasing him the way people tease a chained dog.

Pathan crossed Appu's tea shop and was walking when suddenly he heard, "Hey Pathaaan, don't walk in the middle of the road, make way…" Saying this, one guy threw a plantain skin at him. Pathan stopped in his tracks and turned.

"Go and throw this at your fathers, you bastards…"

"At my father? You can just go to hell…"

Soon, a few more boys joined and there was a ruckus. The betel shop owners and other hawkers on the street joined in laughing at Pathan. Pedestrians on the street stopped just to see what was going on. One old guy who came to buy some tobacco, said, "Get going, boys. Don't you feel sad that he is not well. Just let him be." No one seemed to pay heed to the old man's words. This was considered normal by everyone in the bazaar. It would seem novel only to those coming to the bazaar rarely or for the first time. Even after Pathan had crossed the junction, the boys didn't seem to leave him.

"Hey Pathaaan, do you need sardines? The shop is selling ten sardines for one anna…"

Suddenly, a boy accidentally brushed against Pathan's swollen hand in a sling and ran off.

"Oh God…" Pathan felt as if he was dying. He screamed. He couldn't move an inch. He walked slowly and slumped on the bench outside the rope shop. He could not think of anything else or of taking revenge on any one. The stabbing pain from his hand was the only thing he could focus on. His inner voice nudged him. "You are getting paid for all the crimes that you have committed. This is a lesson for all those who go reckless in their youth."

Pathan, overwhelmed with emotions, carefully caressed his right hand with his left and wailed in pain.

Govindan chased the boys away and came to Pathan. The boys also understood the gravity of Pathan's situation and left, saying they would return next day. Else those boys would not have heeded anyone, not even Govindan.

The rope shop owner and other shop owners went about their

daily business, not bothering about the chaos happening in front of their shops. Hand-carts, bullock-carts, men carrying loads on their heads to shops and delivering goods to houses, women who sat and spun thatches for roof, all went back to their work. Cycle bells, sounds of hawkers selling their wares continued. Heavy duty vehicles like buses and lorries did not enter this street. A white van that evicted beggars from roads came by occasionally. The bazaar went back to its clockwork-like function.

"Pathan, are you crying? Get up. Come let us go. Don't mind these useless fellows. Treat them like barking dogs and just ignore them. Such acts should be condemned. But who can be blamed and who can we go and complain to? Instead, the best thing to do is to just dust yourself and get going. It is the fate of this bazaar that it has to witness such inhumanity. Come on, let's go." Consoling him thus, Govindan helped Pathan to his feet and helped him to his hut. The sight of Govindan supporting Pathan appeared disproportionate; Pathan was a towering figure, while Govindan was scrawny yet sturdy. Slowly, Govindan brought Pathan to his hut, spread a mat and helped him lie down, promised to return with porridge, and left.

Lying down on the mat of his humble hut, Pathan could think of nothing but the acute pain of his right hand. The pain was numbing him everywhere. It was the fifth day today. The doctor had to search for the vein in his hand to administer the injection. The spot where he had been injected was already burning, as if someone had applied chilli paste on it. It was exactly there that the cruel brat had bumped into him. Pathan felt that his heart had stopped that instant. Other than Pathan, no one else would have been able to bear the pain that he was going through. Had it been someone else, they would have killed themselves on Bazaar Street right then.

His eye infection had reduced considerably. The stinging pain from his eyes was also gone. Only when he woke up in the morning, his eyes would be stuck by the dried secretion which had to be removed by washing.

In a corner of his hut, a white bottle hung by a rope. On top of the brick stove was a chimney lamp and match box. His lungi was flung on the trunk box, and the red underwear that he had hung out to dry was stuffed in the roof. A poster of Madhuri Devi and Anjali Devi hugging each other was stuck on the wall. A poster of the old movie Vanamohini, it had yellowed with age. Pathan remembered that he had asked Govindan's son Kuttan to fetch a pot of water. Pathan wondered if the boy had brought the water or not, but could not get up to check. The dosai and gruel that he had at Appu's tea stall that morning remained undigested and he could feel the acid burn in his chest. His hand was more painful than on the previous day.

The more he remained lying down, the more tired he felt. Wishing he would die soon and end his pain and misery, his soliloquy began...

Thinking of this killing pain in my hand, I am not sure that I will even survive once these eight days are over. Instead I just wish I would die now. But I would like to see how this bazaar, these rowdy boys, these shop owners and others are going on. Who doesn't have any wish or desire? Already I cannot walk with my head up in Bazaar Street. It feels like hanging a rat by its tail and teasing it. These are the boys who used to wet their pants just four or five years back at my sight. Now age has caught up with me. Even if I pick up a glass to drink tea, my hands and fingers start shaking. With just six ounces of alcohol, my speech starts to slur and I can't walk straight. Even if I decide not to talk anything, unwanted words make their way to my tongue automatically. My senses have gone out of control. Unlike earlier days, I am not able to just wield a cleaver or even a pen knife. I have to be aware of the police as well. Even if I walk past them, they are asking to blow and test my breath. I have to fear everything.

When I was younger and in my senses, I never had any trouble. No matter what I did, no one dared to ask me anything. "Did Pathan do this? Don't ask him anything. Asking him anything is similar to teasing a sleeping snake, which will only sting you back. It is better to just leave him alone," was the general opinion.

There had been no incidents for a long time. But it was around Muharram of his forty fifth or forty sixth year. Moideen, who worked in the shop up the mound, asked, "Pathan! Would you be interested to play the role of a ferocious tiger?" Why should I even need to think about it? I said yes immediately. For ten days, all that one had to do was to drink and dance like there was no tomorrow. No one to question.

I was the tiger in the street play. That was the time when I killed nine goats with my teeth. It wasn't that long ago. It was on the eighth day. It happened in front of Nair's vessel shop. From Palayam and Bazaar Street, there were a lot of men wearing different masks of various characters and were playing the long drums, horns, and other instruments. There was vigorous dancing to the music.

I was brought before the vessel shop. There was no stopping

the Chenda by Kariyapillai Guru and the drums by Damodaran. They were a pair to reckon with. Kadhar from the shop up the mount wore a tiger mask and came to Bazaar Street. He was drunk. I felt like catching hold of him and smashing him. Like a move to challenge me, he had tiger marks on his back and wore bells on his feet. He started dancing to the beats. As the beats and the volume increased, it felt like a trance. I got up with a start.

I danced like there was no tomorrow. I danced without my feet touching the ground. Kadhar also danced with equal vigour. Slowly, a crowd started gathering. No vehicles or out-station bus could pass through. Buses and cars lined up one behind the other. Folks driving from Arya Salai and Killi Paalam who came asking for the reason of the traffic jam also stood there watching the dance.

Nayar, who owned the vessel shop, had sent for two goats and they had arrived. Each goat stood up to my hip and was as huge as a buffalo. As soon as the goats arrived, one pounce on them, one big bite on the back. With a huge grunt "Mmmeeehhhh" and a loud shout, the goat flew in the air above my head and fell six feet away.

These thoughts only made me think of my current age, my fatigue. The owner of Hotel Ameen was related to Kadhar. He had brought four goats there to use as meat in his hotel. Both the hotel guy and Kadhar wanted to win. I knew it already. As soon as the goats were lined up, I gorged into them without my using my hands. The crowd erupted with applause and whistles. By the end of the hour I had finished nine goats. The police van stopped and the cops stood amongst the crowd to watch. It was not an ordinary crowd. There were as many people as six village carnivals together.

Nayar held my now trunk-like hand and put a one sovereign gold ring on the finger. It seems like long back. It must have been worth forty-five annas then.

Such was my past and these boys are now teasing and making fun of me. Even the same vessel shop Nayar keeps watching all this. All his wealth is equal to the hair on my feet.

"Pathan brother! Pathan brother! Are you sleeping or just lying down?"

When Pathan woke up from his thoughts, it was the liquor shop guy Natarajan standing at the entrance.

"Govindan told me that you have been going to the hospital for the last four or five days. Is that why you don't come to my shop any more in the evenings? Did you know what happened three or four days back? Two new inspectors have come to our station from Kottayam. Along with two other constables, they had come here to the colony. As soon as I saw the cops, I was alert. They surrounded me on all sides. Am I one to give in? Even before they could get to me, I escaped and hid in Madhu's house on the other side of the stream. I heard that they had come till the big stream. Then, when they couldn't get hold of me, they went back and broke all my pots and vessels. I came out only this morning. When I went to my hut, I saw that all my vessels were broken into a dozen pieces. Useless fellows. But thank god, that it was only the vessels that had gone. Had they captured me, I would have had to give them five or ten to get out.

"I heard that the doctor had told you to chop off your hand, Govindan told me. If it is risking your life, just chop it off. I will tell you one thing. From now on, please don't drink that stupid thing. Don't even go near it. I know I am the one selling it. I also know that you don't drink on credit and that you pay me every time. You have also given me change whenever I was short of cash. I will be grateful to you till the end of my life. I have a lot of regards for you, so please avoid it. What are you looking at? You want to go to the toilet? Ok get up slowly. Shall I come with you?"

Pathan did not have the heart to lean on Natarajan, with his stick like legs and his musician-like punk hair-style. But he did not have a choice and he needed support.

Holding Natarajan for support, Pathan went to the toilet. Once he came back, he felt thirsty, so Natarajan poured cold water into a bowl from the mud pot and gave it to him. He asked Pathan if he wanted anything from the tea shop. Pathan asked him for *beedis* for ten paise and gave him the money. Again, he started reminiscing...

Now everyone is taking me for granted. Earlier, or even a week ago, Natarajan would never come near me to talk to me. In retrospect, I have never performed any kind act for any one all these years. If at all I did help someone, it was only because I wanted something in return. I have done a lot of unfaithful and treacherous acts... When I was working in the butcher's shop in the market, I have on more than one occasion flung the cleaver at the dogs waiting for scraps. They would get hit on their tails or backs and howl in pain. They would run away with blood dripping down their bodies while I laughed. In those days it was funny. The ladies who came the bazaar used to scowl at me and say, "Why are you torturing that poor animal? Your hand will definitely become paralyzed." I was never bothered and used to say, "It is ok grandma. If my hand goes numb, I will soak it in salt and pickle it." It was weird that I remember that now, because the doctor administers salt water every day to my hand. Earlier there was a saying that when you commit a crime, you will pay for it in your next birth. Now, times have changed so that you pay for your crimes almost the next day.

It feels like I have been sick and bedridden for almost five or six months now, though it is only the sixth day today. For one who has been roaming in the sun and rain, to sit indoors and be dependent on someone feels like being imprisoned. All I do is sleep, wake up, lie down and sleep again. When I am lying awake, my mind wanders aimlessly to the past and brings up thoughts I had never thought of before.

There was an incident. Thinking about it sends shivers down my spine even now. Just as I cannot forget the incident at the fort house, I cannot forget this incident either. I must have been more than thirty years old that time. I used to wear a black turban and a golden talisman on my biceps and my walk had a gait to it. I had run away from home at the age of fifteen or sixteen and landed first at the butcher's shop… then went to Pathan Chettiyar's shop. Until then, there was no incident worth mentioning in my life. The rainy night at the fort house where I had my first experience as a man… That proved to be lucky as it opened up a lot more opportunities…

I was employed at the bus depot, where all the buses were parked. Nayar's vessel shop had not yet come up. There were a couple of Muslims who had set up shops selling vessels which they bought from Sivadanu Pillai's wholesale shop. Sivadanu's shop always would always be crowded with shopkeepers bringing old used vessels to sell and shopkeepers wanting to buy new brass vessels. At the bus depot, my job was to load and unload the buses that came and went to various places. My very presence was enough. The boys there would do all the work. I would get paid for overseeing. I used to earn four or five coins every day. In Killipaalam, Sivan contractor had a liquor shop. I used to spend half my earnings at his shop. I used to be friends with the Menon who used to do magic on the streets. It was one-of-a-kind friendship.

It was around ten-thirty-one night. From the bus that arrived from Nagercoil at the bus depot, a woman got down. Most of the shops were closed. I had spread a towel on the physician's bench and was lying down. Business that day had not been great, and I was thinking about my empty stomach when that woman got down from the bus. As soon as I saw her, I understood what kind of a woman she was. She was dusky and looked swell. There was nothing to complain about her face either. Her breasts looked well-made and also the bun on her head. She appeared to be over thirty. She wore a double border saree with a matching blouse and painted lips. I jumped with a jerk from the bench and approached her.

"Are you carrying any heavy luggage?" I asked.

She turned and looked at me from top to bottom. The bus went past us and disappeared into the darkness. There were not many people out on the road.

"Luggage? I don't have any luggage. I am the only luggage here. If you want to take me somewhere you are most welcome to do so," she said in a lilting voice.

She was looking for someone to take her and found herself in the company of a very good taker.

I picked her and brought her to the colony that day. I did not reside here then. Back then, I did not have a place of my own. I used to lie down wherever I could, be it the shop bench or someone's house until dawn. The colony was also not like it is now. It was lush and had a thick green cover. Grass as tall as I was, coconut trees, plantain trees, palm trees were abundant. In between were wild shrubs that carpeted the ground. The population was also sparse with families of grass cutters who had settled down. I took the woman straight to the house of Govindan's uncle's house. His uncle worked in the Corporation to catch stray dogs. He was single and did not have a wife or kids. I woke him up that night and told him the news. The street dogs started barking on hearing my footsteps. Frogs were croaking in the fields nearby.

I left her at the uncle's house and came back to the bus depot. I called out to Magic Menon and both of us went to the railway station. We had dinner at a hotel that was open. After dinner, we went to a liquor shop, bought a few bottles of liquor and some meat and reached the uncle's house at one in the night.

I, Govindan's uncle and Menon, the three of us went to sleep with her one after the other. The liquor and the meat gave us such a high that we had no idea what we were doing. The day was dawning and light was starting to show. We were out of alcohol. Despite running out of liquor, I wanted to have one last time with her. When I finished my time with her and woke her up, there was no movement or breath.

She was gone.

She had died.

Now thinking back about that day, I don't feel anything,

because it has been so many years since that happened. Around twenty years or more. What we did at the end was most horrific. It is impossible to do something like that now, with police, police dogs, CID and many things that will sniff out everything you do. It is not easy to escape now. It was easier to escape with whatever we did without even God knowing about it.

As soon as he realized that there was a mishap, Govindan's uncle did not waste time in thinking. He brought the van used to take stray dogs. No one in the colony even knew anything about it. He loaded the body in a box, put it in the van and took it to the place where the stray dogs were killed in an electric chamber. Once the job was done, they buried the body along with the dogs and left.

By the time the sun rose and the day dawned, everything was over. All this was possible because of Govindan's uncle. This Menon used to talk with such high airs when he stood in the ground showing his tricks; but that night, the minute he came to know that the woman was dead, he fled the scene. Later, I saw him at the turning of Chandra Press at his grandmother's house, where he was lying low. Even when I told him all that had happened and convinced that nothing would befall him, he wasn't satisfied. Even Govindan's uncle and I were scared. But no one came in search of the woman and it has been ages since the incident happened. But the very thought of that night chills me to the bone even today.

It is not an act that is done by any ordinary human. Even if such an act was committed, would it be possible for them to roam around others and be self-righteous? Would it be possible for them to talk to others normally? All that was possible those days…

After that I felt scared to go to bus depot and stopped going there altogether.

When my father was alive – he used to speak in Hindi. I am not very fluent in Hindi. If someone talks I can understand but I would not be able to reply. My father's name was Hameembhai. Everyone knew Hameembai who used to paint tiger masks on people during street plays. He had a notable personality just like me. He was not of dark complexion like me though… I was the only dark-complexioned person in my house. My father's relatives used to call me 'Kaala' which means 'black' in Hindi. My father cursed me that I would suffer and decay and die. That was because when he came home once fully drunk, I smashed him so hard that he fell like a felled tree trunk. I ran away from home after hitting my father, so I had no home, no place to call my home, no siblings… nothing…

Next to Parameshwar Iyer's hut was a stone quarry that was the end of the road after the director's office. It was well-known as Pathan Quarry. That was the name of my house as well. My father, myself and my two sisters were the four members of the house. My mother had died young. With heavy earrings adorning her ears, white stoned nose-ring, polka dotted saree, and a dusky complexion, I could recall my mother only as a shadow and do not remember much of her. It is difficult to remember much from the age of five or six. But my eyes still well up when thinking of her.

My father was a painter. The house had a stone to grind the paint and there were worn out brushes stuffed in the thatched roof. Each wall had paint of a different colour splashed on it. Every time you entered the house, it smelled of varnish. The inner wall had tiger masks and decorating accessories hanging from a nail. Looking at the mask with its pointed ears, red tongue sticking out and red eyes, anyone would be scared to even enter the room.

We were always starved at home and went to bed with stomachs half full. Both my sisters stayed at home and sold pancakes, which constituted the major share of the family income. Fish and roots were our staple diet. Rarely, when there was extra income, we had gruel or rice. But being the youngest in the house, my sisters made sure I got the first two pancakes every day before they were sold. My father did not have painting jobs every day. Even if he did, whatever he earned was spent on himself and his drinking. If he did give some money to the house, it had to be fish and rice for dinner that day, else both my sisters will have to suffer the scoldings and the thrashing that came their way.

During Muharram, work was abundant thanks to the street plays. There was no one better at painting masks than my father. People acting in street plays came from the bazaar, other colonies, and even far off villages to get their faces and bodies painted during Muharram. Jagathi Ameem Bai was a very famous name as a painter.

During those days I had a job. After the actors shaved their entire bodies, my job was the daub varnish on their torsos before my father painted on them. During the period of Muharram, the house was filled with chicken meat, alcohol and different coloured paints.

My father would have been around seventy years old then and I was around fifteen years. There was a single woman who lived in the portion below us. There was word around town that she was not of good character. She looked good and she always smelled of talcum powder. I liked her. Whenever I was home she used to call me, "Kaala, come here, I will pick the lice from your head." She would make me sit on her lap and caress my head. It was comforting. "What lice is she going to find in your bald head? Don't go to that bitch's house, Kaala," my sisters would scold. Her name was Bangi. Bangi always gave me something to snack on. Once I dreamt that Bangi and I were riding on a scooter together.

Some folks in the colony spoke openly about how Bangi and my father were in a relationship. I also came to know that my father was staying some nights with her and also giving her money. With two grown girls of marriageable age, at the age of seventy, he was acting as if he was still young and sleeping around with that woman. From the moment I learnt about my father's relationship with Bangi, it made me cringe. I wanted to show my rage and was waiting for the opportune moment. While my sisters were toiling hard at home and trying to make ends meet, my father was sleeping around with someone and spending all his money on her.

One day, I saw my father leave Bangi's house and climb the stairs to our house. It must have been close to midnight and he was drunk. I was seething in anger; as soon as he sat down, I hit him with a thick rod. He fell down with a thud and cursed me. "You will die a sorry death."

That was the day I left my house. After that I even erased the fact that I had two sisters and a father from my memory.

—

It was around dusk when Pathan stepped out of the house. Govindan's wife Paachi was looking at him slowly coming out.

"Pathan brother, where are you going alone at this time?" she asked.

"I want to relieve myself first. After that I will go to Appu's tea shop. The gruel that Govindan gave in the afternoon is untouched in the same place. If it remains there it will go bad. So please take it Paachi."

"Didn't you drink the gruel?"

"No. I didn't drink it in the afternoon as I had dozed off. Now I feel like having a tea."

"Why do you have to strain yourself with this hand? Can't you send Kuttan to fetch something for you?"

"It is not possible to give this hand as an excuse and remain indoors Paachi. I want to go to the toilet and relieve myself. I have to get up for that and I have to go alone for that. Can you please light a lamp inside the chimney?"

"Ok brother, go and come back. I will light a lamp."

Pathan walked past the temple in Elavaaniya street. The temple bells chimed for the evening prayers. He began talking to himself.

I could not sleep at night no matter how much I tried. I could not sleep during the day either. If I force my eyes shut, all the old thoughts keep chasing me. My old memories keep boiling inside of me like bubbles forming in hot water. To relive my past as if I am narrating it as a story to someone else feels calming. It has become dark now. I do not know the time. The brass lamp that Paachi lit has now run out of oil and is now burning up in smoke. The flame is dying and there are insects flying around it. I think it might be mosquitoes. I was lying buried under the sheet and could not feel the mosquito bites. The umbrella repairman Muhammad and his wife are talking something amongst themselves. God knows what they are talking.

The sambar and dosai that I had from Appu's tea shop is still undigested and feels like acid burning in my chest.

After hitting my father, I ran away from home and reached the bazaar junction straightaway. My hand was not swollen like this then. Only the top of my arm had a swelling like a small gooseberry. Over the years, the swelling kept increasing. Due to neglect, it has now swollen like an elephant's trunk. All these days there was no pain or discomfort in my hand.

When I had gone to take a bath in the nearby stream, I remember having been pierced by a thorn. Only when it got infected and the pain became unbearable, did I even go to the doctor. He said that my hand should be amputated after taking injections for eight days. Lorry cleaner Unni's hand was cut off after a lorry accident. His left hand was cut off below the elbow. From now, I should also walk with a towel around my body. I can't even imagine the teasing and the mocking of the bazaar boys. But after my hand is removed, the stub will heal and my left hand will gain the strength of my right hand. Then I will take my revenge on those useless boys. Just a few more days. Let those dogs bark all they want.

After I ran away from my house, I walked for more than three miles and reached Bazaar Street at the vegetable shop junction. I was walking and roaming around the area over the next few days, when the vegetable vendor Suppan Chettiyar called out to me.

That was the time when this bazaar – the carpenter, the fort house, the mound, the nearby places like Surakkadu Paalayam, Killipaalam, Buddhankottai, the fort on the East side, Gandhi Hotel lane, the ground, the fruit market, Wednesday Bazaar – these were all unknown. The buses would keep plying between different places, and there was constant incoming traffic, buses from and to Neyaatrangarai – Thakkalai – Thoduvatti – Nagercoil would stop at the butcher's shop junction. In buses that arrived from eight in the morning to noon, there would be baskets and baskets of vegetables. Suppan Chettiyar had appointed me to keep an eye on Mastan who unloaded the vegetable baskets from the buses, so that he did not steal the brinjals and the yams to sell them on the side. It was the job that I landed on the second day I ran away from home, because Suppan Chettiyar took pity on me.

His house was located in the laundry street where all the rich people's clothes were washed by washer men. I had to go there to collect his lunch at noon every day. I had to walk in the hot sun for more than a mile. Nowadays, even boys who cannot walk properly are cycling past. In those days there were not many cycles or buses that plied to that side of the city. Moreover, I did not even know how to ride a cycle. I have travelled by train, ship and also taken a ride in scooters. But never learnt how to ride a cycle. To learn to ride a cycle is akin to a circus act. Balancing oneself on two wheels is definitely an act. Nowadays, kids are riding cycles confidently as fast as a scooter.

I worked at Chettiyar's shop for almost two years. Meanwhile, someone had gone and told my father that I was working at the bazaar and he came and called me home twice. The first time it was my sister's wedding. I didn't go. I had made a vow not to go there and I stuck to it. Whenever I think of my vow, I think of Bangi. The way she caressed my hair and the way she smelled of talcum powder is nostalgic. Yet, I stuck to my vow and did not back. I heard the news that both my sisters were married to another Pathan who worked at the government office in the city. After that I did not have any reason to go home. My mother had died, my sisters had left the house after they got married. I did not have any attachment to my father and did not go back. I did not have a house or anyone to call my own. I had even forgotten my mother tongue. From now until I breathe my last, this bazaar is my home.

On one occasion, I stole something from Suppan Chettiyar's shop. Chettiyar had asked me to oversee the shop and had gone out, maybe to the toilet I guess. The cash box was kept outside. It was always filled with brass and silver coins. There was a silver coin on top of the box after a customer bought a plantain. I looked around and couldn't see Chettiyar anywhere. There was no one in the next shop also. I took the coin and put it in my mouth immediately. After a while, when Chettiyar returned, I do not know how he found out. But as soon as he came, he gave me a ripe fruit and asked me to eat it. I took the fruit and told him that I will eat later and kept it in my hand. "Eat it now, why it won't enter your stomach now? Did you just eat an elephant?" demanded Chettiyar. How could I eat? I had the coin in my mouth. If I turned around to spit it out, Chettiyar would not allow me to turn around. I had no other go, so I spat out the coin in front of him.

"Where did you get this money from?" he asked. I did not lie to him. I told him that I saw it on top of the cash box and took it, hoping that he might let me go for my honesty. But he asked me to get out. Chettiyar did not like lies and thieves. He was a famous person then. He looked as white as a pumpkin and well-built. He used to wear a crisp white dhoti and a towel on top. He never had any hair on his head and was always bald. He wore a Rudraksh that he had got from Pazhani temple around his neck. His forehead was always smeared with sacred ash. He had made big money with this look and he stuck to it.

He owned a row of eight houses in the dhobi street. I have also heard that he had land and houses somewhere in the east – in Tuticorin. He was also the vegetable supplier to the prison contractor. That was another good source of income. Even though he was rich, he was an honest man. As soon as the goods were delivered he always paid for them. He did not live on credit. Unlike a lot of other sellers, he did not argue with the vendors about the quality of vegetables – brinjals are bad, potatoes are old, etc. He was also a generous man. If anyone came to his doorstep and asked for money or food, he never sent them back empty-handed. He took me under him, and stitched me a set of clothes – a pair of khaki shorts and a vest. Even if it was a small chili, if you asked him for one, he would give you five. He did not entertain lies or theft. Just one small impulsive act, and I ruined everything.

After that incident, I joined Pathan Chettiyar's provision store tactfully. No one would be able to say that we were both Pathans, so he favoured me. Such was our relationship. While working in his shop, I went to deliver goods to the house in the fort and had my first experience with a woman, I must have been around nineteen years old. Only after that did I become arrogant. After that, I felt that the whole bus depot and the bazaar were in my control. Then I worked at the butchers. At the tea shop. I have sold oranges. That was the time when I was at my peak and my gang was the most formidable. My gang was myself and the magician Menon only. I recently heard that Menon had settled somewhere in Madras or Bombay with a Nair woman.

Menon was quite a fair and well-built guy. But he was also quite shrewd and sly. He must have been around thirty-five years old and was forever thirty-five. He would shave every day. He always wore linen full-sleeved shirts with crisp white dhotis. Any woman who went past him turned to give him a second glance. He used to sleep like a log, without knowing anything around, then suddenly be fully awake and fully alert and gather huge crowds at the city ground under the huge banyan tree. "Come one, come all! Are your eyes telling the truth or are they lying? If you are able to find out, take it all! No fake, no cheating! Come and get mesmerized!" Hearing this, the crowds would get wooed and gather around him. Tooth powder and oil made by himself sold to the crowds like hot cakes. I first met Menon while on my delivery route while working at Chettiyar's provision store. I stood surprised in the same place after watching his magic show. I stood till the crowd had dispersed.

Then, when we were alone, Menon tapped me on the shoulder and asked, "You liked the magic, my friend? Can you spare a *beedi*?" he asked. I was surprised that a guy as well-dressed as him was asking me for a *beedi*. It was only later after I moved with him, I came to know that he was a totally different person on the inside than on the outside. He was the one who took me to Rukmini's house for my one-night stand. After that we were both a team. As soon as the sun set, our fun would begin. We were a team both in terms of money and when it came to sharing women. But after we killed the woman we had met at the bus stop, we stopped meeting each other. I inquired with his grandmother, who said it was ages since she saw him. After a while, I just gave up on his friendship.

I heard a cock crow somewhere, which was followed by more crowing everywhere, near and far.

—

"Looks like it has dawned. That is why I am wide awake," thought Pathan. He tried moving his right hand and felt he could move it without feeling pain. He removed the cloth which supported his right hand from his neck. He moved his fingers and they moved.

"I don't feel the pain anymore. The swelling and the pus have also reduced considerably. The doctor is a shrewd man. He said that he will be able to ascertain the status of my hand only after eight days. Tomorrow is the eighth day. If the Gods take pity on me, I would be able to save my hand. I have lived with a swollen hand till now. I can survive the rest of my life with this hand. I wish my prayers would be answered. I have never gone to the mosque even once. Never taken up a fast or even said my daily prayers. I have been to a prayer gathering during Muharram with my father as a child. That was only for the feast and to see the festivities of Muharram where people walked on fire as penance. After that, I never even thought about God. Then how can I expect God to answer my prayers?" The day was going to dawn, and Pathan felt sleepy. He pulled his dhoti above his head and dozed off.

Even at eight in the morning there was a long queue of

patients who had taken tokens to see the doctor. The peon was first sending those who had to go to their offices or factories. Each patient went inside the doctor's cabin, and after consultation took their prescriptions to the dispensary behind the clinic.

Pathan could not stand in the queue with his arm in a sling, so he stood leaning on a pillar. He had a short stubble, the growth of the past seven days, and the look of not having bathed for almost five days. Even at this stage, the sturdy look on his face was apparent. Since the pain had reduced from the previous day, Pathan felt relieved. Very eager to hear the doctor's words, he was leaning on the pillar waiting for his turn, fearing that someone might brush against his arm. The peon had said that he would be allowed only after the crowd had considerably reduced.

As he waited, the crowd and the queue only grew in size. Finally, when the peon called out to Pathan, it was past ten o clock.

The doctor, bent over his desk, was writing when Pathan entered. He looked up and smiled at Pathan. "Your eight days are over today. I hope you are happy now. Come closer and let me see your arm. Remove the cloth sling and see if you can stretch the hand."

"Yes I can stretch my hand now."

"That is because you followed my instructions and did not drink alcohol for the last eight days. It is seen in your hand. Stretch and flex your hand a couple of times. I will give another injection now. One more thing. Your hand need not be amputated, so you need not worry. But that does not mean you can go back to your old ways. However, I will give you tablets that you need to take one daily for the next thirty days. If I prescribe tablets, do you have money to buy them?"

"How much will those tablets cost?"

"Fifteen rupees. Do you have the money? Would you be able to buy?"

"Yes, I have the money."

"You don't need the sling support any longer. You can lower your hand and be normal. Keep stretching and flexing your hand as much as possible. Remember, no alcohol. If you go back to drinking, I will not give any guarantee for your hand. Understand? You can go now."

Pathan took the prescription from the doctor and bowed silently thanking him profusely.

"If you really want to thank me, just follow my instructions. I will see you later."

Syed Pathan saw heaven before his eyes. He slowly lowered his right hand. It felt a little heavy and he realized it would take some time for him to walk fast. "As long as the doctor did not chop off my hand, it doesn't matter how fast I walk. But the doctor is a sly man. He blew up a small thing into a big mountain and scared the hell out of me. It was a good thing though, else I would not have kept quiet with this swollen hand also. I would have definitely had a few drinks a couple of times to forget the pain."

As he got down from the clinic and started walking on the

road, he felt his hand aching above the elbow. In the high-school grounds, students were performing their drills. He walked to the end of the street and turned. Once he turned, he could see the shed of the kings and the chariot base from afar. The street had all the big houses that were part of the palace which were empty and wore a sullen silent look. Life insurance companies now had their offices in some of the premises close to the palace, premises that had earlier housed chariot riders and other employees. He crossed all these grand empty houses and crossed the fort house where he had his first encounter with a woman. He felt nothing now. Much time had passed. All that stood of the old bungalow was the huge decorated door, now dull and its paint peeling off. Even the jackfruit tree no longer existed and all that could be seen above the shut door was just emptiness.

As Pathan neared the fruit stall near the Ganapathy temple, he felt the pain in his arm increase. He felt it would be more comfortable if he kept it folded. So he took his towel and folded his arm and put it in a sling like before. He knew it had not healed completely, which was the reason why the doctor had given pills for a month. He had to continue to be careful. He had suffered enough for his lifetime over the last eight days, so he would not let it get to him now.

Even though it was almost noon, it was not hot. The sky looked like it might rain in the evening.

Pathan crossed the streets one by one; as soon as he reached the bazaar, he felt a slight pain in his chest. He thought that if he walked further, he might spot some of the local boys in the bazaar. Or maybe they had all gone for some work at this time of the day.

"I should just cross this bazaar and reach my place without anyone seeing me," thinking thus, he walked along the side of the road.

No matter how much Pathan tried to hide himself and walk along the side of the road, his height gave him away. He could be easily spotted from far away even in a crowded street.

As he was nearing the Sannadi junction, two boys standing at the betel shop spotted him.

"Hey! Pathan is coming this way. Hey Pathan, where are you coming from?" called out one boy in a baritone voice and ran off in the lane adjacent to Appu's tea shop.

Pathan did not want to turn and look but out of habit, he turned to look. As soon as he turned, the towel fell loose and gave way, leaving his hand exposed.

"Hey! Pathan's hand is healed now. Be careful, else he will just throw us all with that hand."

"Yes, you bloody rascals. I have come to whack you and throw you all," the rage that he had kept controlled over the last eight days erupted. One of the boys picked up a stone and threw it at Pathan which hit his right elbow.

"Aaaaaaaaa…"

Pathan collapsed and sat down. One of the boys grabbed Pathan's towel and ran away; another came and pushed him down.

The betel shop owners and other hawkers guffawed at this scene in front of their shops.

The sun, which was faint until now, shone brightly. Pathan felt a sharp pain in his chest. The sharp pain slowly went to his head, before he could realize or react to it.

Pathan's corpse lay on the road with his eyes wide open at the sun!

—

Ummini

Ummini was sound asleep on the bench in front of the tobacco shop, covered from head to toe with his dirty *dhoti,* curled up like a foetus. The ground was swarming with flies and it was close to eight in the morning. The sun had risen; the shops on Bazaar Street were opening their shutters one by one. The morning sun touched Ummini's feet. Though he was awake, he felt lazy to get up. Govindan cleared the gutter with his rake and reached the tobacco shop. Seeing that Ummini's big toe was moving, he gathered the garbage with his rake and kept it on the stone near Ummini's head.

"Hey Ummini! Hasn't it dawned for you yet? This stench is so unbearable that my insides might come out any minute and here you are rolling around as if it smells like a bed of flowers. Wake up!"

Ummini yawned and stretched his whole body under the

dhoti. From under the cover, he lifted his head slightly and looked at Govindan standing with his rake.

"What are you looking at? Get up, you lazy bugger!" Govindan shouted at him. Ummini stood up with a jerk and the *dhoti* fell down, exposing Ummini in all his naked glory. He picked up the cloth hurriedly before Govindan could spank him with the rake and tied it to his skinny waist. Ummini, with his hollowed cheeks, droopy sour eyes, wide face and unruly hair looked around while scratching his head, pondering over which place would be acceptable for passing urine. If he pissed in the gutter when Govindan was still around, his morning would not go well. Though Ummini was scared of Govindan and his long rake, his day began only when Govindan scolded him and woke him up every morning. In case Ummini was in deep sleep and didn't wake up on the first call, the rake would fall on his head. So he decided it would be better not rub Govindan on the wrong side.

"Go Ummini, the big houses are waiting for you. Go and get something to eat or drink. The day has begun. Not that you have anything important to do. The ladies of the houses will be waiting for you with their porridge. What is there for you to worry about? You don't have a house or children to worry about. Go on. Get going."

Ummini yawned loudly while stretching his arms, rubbed his eyes and looked at Govindan with his usual stained-teeth smile.

"Don't show me your dirty teeth. How long has it been since you brushed your teeth? Swine!" Govindan muttered to himself and continued pulling garbage out of the gutter with his rake. Ummini waited for Govindan to turn the corner and go out of sight. As soon as his head turned, Ummini sat on the gutter's edge and relieved himself. He got up and thought about his next plan of action for the day. He scratched his head vigorously and spat out loud. With the gait of someone with a plan, he started walking towards the carpenter's house in the upper-class street. From outside he shouted, "Anyone home? Do you have food for me? Ummini has come."

"Look at him coming early in the morning. Like a guest as if we have food on the stove waiting for him to be served. Wait. My hands are busy." Thus shouted the lady of the house from inside. He smiled back and stood there. Feeling something crawl on his back, he tried to reach it but couldn't. He brushed it off with the towel in his hand, and tied his dhoti tighter around his waist. The lady of the house came out with a pan of the previous day's rice gruel and gave him a leaf.

"Ummini, don't run away after you drink this. I have kept the brush and bleaching powder. Wash and clean the toilets. Understood?"

Ummini nodded, while concentrating on the gruel being poured on the leaf.

Ummini was always welcome in any high-rise house of the upper-class street. He was fed and also given a task which he happily performed. Once his morning ritual was done, he walked around the bazaar and the main streets as if he owned them. He would go to the betel shop, get two betel leaves with a nut to chew on. With the betel leaves in his mouth, he was walking by the metal shops and an old shopkeeper called out, "Hey Ummini, fill this pot with water. Take this lemon peel, scrub the pot clean of all the mud, then fill it. Don't put your hand in the water. Once you come back, look what I have saved for you. It is quite ripe and very tasty." The old man showed a fruit and Ummini smiled in happiness.

"Hey Ummini, don't show this smile to everyone. The women who come to the bazaar are bound to fall for you," said Kuttappan the load carrier sarcastically.

It was past ten in the morning, when business in the bazaar was in full glory. All the shops had opened and had kept their wares outside. It would be eleven am when other traders arrived by buses from other towns. Until then Ummini, would be roaming the bazaar or sitting with other load carriers as they gathered in the lane adjacent to Sakkubai's shop, listening to the local barber. The barber would sit and read *Kerala Kaumidhi*. Once the barber started reading the newspaper, his voice would change into a baritone and he would start reading as if he was reciting a sermon. To Kuttappan, Ummini and to those who could not read, the barber was the political guru. Though Ummini could not understand what the barber was reading or comprehend it, he liked the way the barber's moustache danced and the way his mouth swayed when he pronounced the words. Ummini just stood there with his mouth agape.

"Hey Ummini, light this beedi and come," either Kuttappan or Baasha would give him some work. With his usual smile, Ummini would half-heartedly leave.

"Hey Ummini, come let us go and wash the buffaloes," Gopalan the cowherd would call out. It would be past eleven or eleven-thirty by then. Ummini and Gopalan would drive the cattle to the pond. As they reached Arya Road junction, the devotees of

Bhaktanandar Ashram would cross them singing hymns, with their yellow triangular flags as they returned to their ashram carrying their bowls and their morning collection of rice and vegetables. As they sang "Hare Rama Hare Krishna" Ummini would giggle loudly and sarcastically chant, "Ade Rama Ade Krishna" loudly to his own tune. The devotees, unaware of Ummini's gimmicks, would continue to walk towards their ashram.

"Hey Ummini, don't tease the gurus. We do not want to incur their wrath," Gopalan would scold him. Ummini would turn and smile in his usual manner. He did not know anything other than the bazaar that had been his home for as long as he could remember.

Ummini did not have anyone to call his own. He did not own anything. Even his name was not his own. He came to be called Ummini because he had to be called something. No one knew how old he was. Even during the era of C.P. when *Pattam Dhanupillai* was protesting, Ummini was wandering around in Bazaar Street. Ummini had been part of the bazaar and this part of the town for as long as one could remember. He was called Ummini by all, young and old. His rag-like dhoti, stained teeth, unkempt hair, innocent smile and sleepy eyes – this was Ummini even in those days. He never bathed, never brushed his teeth, never owned a piece of clothing, and never had anything to call his own. Yet the world belonged to him. This was Ummini.

He roamed Bazaar Street, the town grounds and other main streets, picking up *beedi* stubs and smiling at everyone until the last show was over at night. During the day he slept on the steps of the Padmanabha temple tank, or stared until sunset at the bats hanging upside down from the trees. At night, he came and slept on the bench outside the tobacco shop. With his head cloth, he would dust the bench, cover himself from head to toe with his *dhoti*, and sleep. Once he fell asleep, not even a bolt of thunder, heavy rain or even a cyclone could wake him up. Only when the morning sun touched his face would Ummini wake up. Else it would be Govindan or the sweeper Chellamma who would have to wake him.

"One should live life like Ummini. Even a million rupees cannot bring that state of mind. He must be blessed to live such a carefree life."

It was in the wee hours, past one or two at night, when Ummini came to sleep one night. He had attended the wedding night in one of the big houses of the upper-class street and gorged on a big feast for lunch. Different types of starters, varieties of rice and desserts were served, items that he had never tasted in his life. He lay down and sniffed his hand to see if the aroma still lingered. After the sumptuous feast, he had slept under the big tree at Sannadhi junction and dozed off. He slept around noon and woke up by about five in the evening. It was because of that afternoon siesta that he could not sleep at night.

He tossed and turned, but could not sleep. He felt like singing.

Buzz Buzz Buzz
Sing the mosquitoes
Buzzing by my ears
Keeping me company
In this dark night

He sang whatever came to his mind with a tune of his own. He tried lying on his stomach. He rolled on the cold stone bench.

He felt ants biting on his back. He immediately got up, dusted the bench and his back with his dhoti and again tried to sleep. A dog was howling in the distance. Insects were swarming around the street light. Other than this, there was not a soul in sight. Ummini lay still, trying hard to sleep.

Suddenly he thought he heard a sound. He lay still, fearing that it was an animal.

"Come here. There is place here," said a woman's voice.

"Looks like someone is sleeping there," said a man's deep voice.

"It is just Ummini. He is sound asleep. Nothing will wake him up now. Not even if a bowl of hot water poured on him. Come soon," said the woman's voice.

Silence! Ummini slowly pulled the cloth from his face and peeked out. When he saw the sight before him, he froze. He felt edgy… His mouth started salivating suddenly. The hair all over Ummini's body stood on its ends. He turned and coiled into a fetal position.

"He is turning. He seems to be awake," said the man.

"Let him turn. He is a dumb. Now concentrate and let us finish what we came here for." The woman's voice was quivering, but still focused on the task at hand.

Ummini could not sleep a wink that night no matter how hard he tried. But he had weird thoughts, improper thoughts that would not let him sleep.

Ummini was already up when the milkman brought milk

early next morning. His body covered with his dhoti from below his neck, sitting on the bench, he was rocking back and forth when the milkman crossed the tobacco shop.

Surprised, the milkman asked, "Hey Ummini, looks like the day has dawned early for you today. What happened? You did not sleep?"

Ummini could not reply, but displayed his stained teeth smile. The milkman did not reply as he had a long distance to cover and milk to deliver. He pedaled his cycle and vanished in the darkness.

The whole day, Ummini was in a trance. He went to one of the houses on the upper-class street and ate whatever they gave without even realizing what he was eating. He went about the day like a doll that had been wound up to dance. After breakfast, he directly went and sat down amongst the crowd listening to the barber reading the newspaper. His mind was elsewhere.

"Did you know Ummini, a boat collapsed in the river yesterday… fifteen people died. Good riddance! We can save a lot from the ration like rice and dal," said the barber. Ummini did not heed what was being said. He was in another world. The happenings that he had witnessed the previous night at close quarters never left his mind.

When the fisherwoman Chellamma went past him, he stared at her. When girls went past him to Vijaya Mohini flour mill, he looked at their breasts and backs without even batting his eyes.

"Hey look at Ummini. He is ogling all the girls in our town," Kuttappan called out loudly.

"Get lost, you useless fellows, Leave him alone. Don't drag

him into your tricks and spoil him. He is an innocent guy. Let him be." The barber shouted at Kuttappan and others who mocked at Ummini and laughed at him. But even those who sat in the crowd felt that something was not normal with Ummini that day.

"What happened Ummini? Are you not feeling well? Are you having fever? Here, take this money, go to the pharmacist and buy some tablet for yourself. Go and have a tea," said the metal scrap dealer, giving him ten paise. Ummini went to the village pond with the money. He didn't drink tea or buy medicines. He just sat at the steps watching women bathe. He stood there until the sun rose and it became too hot for him to stand. Later, he went to the local theatre and stood at the entrance watching the women who passed by. Ummini did not feel hunger or thirst. He didn't know what had come over him and he could not express what he felt.

He couldn't sleep as well as he used to. He kept waking up in the middle of the night, looked at the cement bench next to him, reliving the happenings of that night. He spent the night scratching his body and staring into the dark. Even when he tried to sleep, he was woken up by erotic thoughts which he was unable to comprehend. He curled up, kept his hands in between his thighs and tried to sleep. Thus, did he spend his days and nights in loneliness and with those thoughts.

Early one morning, Ummini was in deep sleep, covered from head to toe on his usual bench outside the tobacco shop. The milkman passing by the shop stopped in his tracks on seeing the dead body of a newborn baby, still umbilical cord attached to it, kept near Ummini's head. Ummini, unaware of this, was sleeping. Soon, word spread and a crowd gathered. The women who had come out to fetch water returned home in fear. Word spread far and wide and the whole town was gathered that morning outside the tobacco shop. Amidst all this, Ummini was still asleep. The news had crept into the police station and a police van arrived. A constable took a stick and smacked Ummini right on his feet, who woke up with a start.

Seeing the police and huge crowd looking at him early in the morning, Ummini was puzzled and didn't realize his dhoti had fallen to the ground. "Idiot! Tie your *dhoti* around your waist, shameless fellow," shouted the constable. Hurriedly Ummini picked up the dhoti, tied it around his waist and blinked at everyone.

"Who did this?" bawled the policeman. It was only when Ummini looked in the direction that the policeman's finger was pointing, did he understand why the huge crowd had gathered there early that morning.

Someone in the crowd said, "It was not there when I was returning from the last show of the movie last night. Ummini was also not sleeping on the bench at that time."

"Without this guy knowing, no one would have kept the body here," shouted the inspector.

"He is innocent. He doesn't know anything. He means no harm to anyone." said a bystander.

"Innocent? Who? This guy? He will not answer when I ask. He will answer when my cane talks. He has been here the whole night and you are saying he doesn't know who kept the infant's body here. Come here, you sloth," called out the inspector.

Ummini struggled to answer the inspector's questions. "When

did you come and lie down here? What time was it? Did you see or hear anyone?" he raised his cane while talking to Ummini.

"I don't know. I... here..." he looked at the crowd behind the inspector, hoping someone would speak for him or support him.

"What are you looking at? You don't know? I will see what you know and what you don't know. You will remember everything when I take you to the station and make you vomit the truth. 403! Put him in the van."

It took a couple of hours for the report to be processed. An outline was drawn in the place where the infant's body was found. The body was wrapped in a leaf and sent for post mortem. The weight, height, colour, birthmarks of the infant was noted along other details. The milkman was questioned for details of how and when he spotted the infant on the bench. Signatures of eye witnesses from the crowd were taken on the report and the inspector asked the crowd to disperse. Ummini was taken to the station for further interrogation.

As the van departed, the crowd looked at Ummini sadly. The Bhaktanandar Ashram devotees were returning from their morning rituals. They seemed unperturbed by the crowd and the chaos and continued on their way. Ummini looked at them with tears in his eyes.

As soon as the police van left, everyone started voicing their opinions.

"Poor guy, what does he know? Why did the police have to take him?"

"He is innocent and that is why the police took him. There were so many other men in this crowd. Did they ask anyone else any question? They have their own reason for everything. How do we know to which bitch this child belonged to? The poor child is dead and our poor Ummini is facing the consequences."

The crowd dispersed.

Around five in the evening, Ummini is seen limping on the road from the fort. Kuttappan was the first to see him. Soon a crowd had gathered around Ummini as word spread and people wanted to get a glimpse of him. Whether good or bad, whether it concerned them or not, the people of the bazaar gathered around for everything. The barber, tea shop owner, cobbler, metal scrap dealer everyone had questions for Ummini.

"Hey Ummini, what did they do to you?"

"Look at his face and his back. He has been beaten black and blue. The inspector must have vented all his personal anger and vengeance on our poor Ummini. They have broken his teeth too!" The crowd felt sorry for him.

Someone brought tea without milk for him. Ummini took the tea glass with both hands and sipped the hot tea slowly. He smiled his usual smile at everyone.

"Don't smile, Ummini. Even after so much suffering you are still smiling. It is making me feel terrible. Forget what happened. Looks like you just escaped something big. Now drink this tea. Those ruthless cops couldn't show their anger on anyone else, so they had to show it on you. Those constables and their faces!" murmured the barber.

"Tomorrow we shall write about it in *Kerala Kaumidhi*. We shall all sign a petition and send it to them stating the injustice that has happened to our Ummini. The police will also realize that Ummini is not alone and he has us," said the metal shop owner.

"Why didn't you say anything this morning when the cops were questioning him or when they dragged him to the police station? You could have told them not to take Ummini."

"Do you think the inspector was in any mood to listen to anyone who spoke this morning? Even if I did, he would have slapped the crime on me, claimed that I was the father of the dead infant, and dragged me to the station. That is how they are."

"Let him be. He has had a rough day. Give him some breathing space." The crowd dispersed and Ummini just sat there alone.

After that incident, Ummini became a different man. He no longer slept on the bench outside the tobacco shop. Wherever he found space, he would lie down. He no longer went asking for food at anyone's house. If someone took pity on him and fed him gruel or tea, he accepted happily. Even when the barber read from the newspaper he just stood aloof without sitting amongst the crowd. When given a task, he did without any enthusiasm and seeming half asleep. He became very slow. People took pity on him and gave him an overripe fruit or a tea without milk which he accepted.

"Ummini is a changed person after his visit to the police station. He is not the old Ummini we all knew. His gait and his old enthusiasm are all gone. Look at him now. It is sad to look at him like this," said Kuttappan.

Suddenly, Ummini seemed to have disappeared from the

bazaar. No one remembered seeing him anywhere. People thought that the police had taken him again. Or maybe he was taken away by the orphanage. Or maybe he fell down the steps of the pond and drowned. But if he had died, someone would have seen his body. Not a single soul knew his whereabouts. Each one had their own explanation for Ummini disappearing suddenly.

Gradually Ummini faded away from the minds of the houses, the bazaar, the tea shop, the temple tank, the buffaloes, the Kuttappans, and the barber. Just as Ummini was slowly being forgotten, he reappeared.

Not as the old Ummini, but as a new and revamped Ummini!

On Friday, the devotees of Bhaktanandar Ashram were returning to the ashram with bags of rice and copper vessels containing the alms collected. The last person in the line of devotees, wearing a yellow printed towel bearing the ashram's flags and slogans, head clean shaven and body smeared with holy ash was Ummini!

"*Hare Rama Hare Krishna*
Krishna Krishna Hare Hare!!!"

The parade of devotees crossed Sannadhi junction and went towards their ashram, and Ummini went along with them. The whole bazaar stood and watched with their mouths agape!

About the Translator:

Sandhya Raman:

Born and brought up in Chennai, Tamil Nadu, Sandhya is an engineer by qualification but has added many a feather to her cap over the years. An ever-curious mind, looking for new experiences, she has dabbled in theatre as an actor, writer and director.

Currently working in media, her fluency in both Tamil and English has given her the opportunity to translate and write in both the languages.

Her short list of works includes subtitling, screenplays and translations of various literary works.

She loves the outdoors be it swimming or playing a sport. Sandhya resides in Chennai with her husband, and when she is not surrounded by dogs she is off to explore some new place.

www.ingramcontent.com/pod-product-compliance
Ingram Content Group UK Ltd.
Pitfield, Milton Keynes, MK11 3LW, UK
UKHW040032200726
13854UKWH00001B/479